BAROSSA LILY

randomly

we acknowledge
the deep spirit of country

the land and sky
breathing as one

waters flowing
with stories waiting

trees and rocks
holding memories

songs and stories and art
binding past to present

the wisdom of ancestors
guiding the way

future footsteps
echoing with reverence

© Heather Anne Gordon: 2023: October 14

HEATHER ANNE GORDON

This print edition published in 2025 by
Centred in Choice

*Sharing Australian voices, stories,
strategies and skills with the world.*

Title: Barossa Lily – randomly
Author: Heather Anne Gordon
verses written between 2000 - 2025

First published by Centred in Choice
    ABN 17 601 690 975

Cover Design:
Heather Anne Gordon
mixed media on canvas

Internal Design:
Karen Marree Engel

First Reader:
Gayle Hull Mather

A catalogue record for this book
is available from the National Library of
Australia

ISBN 978-1-7635635-1-3

Author: Heather Anne Gordon

Title: Barossa Lily - randomly

Acknowledgements:

We acknowledge and respect the deep
spiritual connection and the relationship
that First Nations people have to Country.

Country takes in everything within the
landscape – landforms, waters, air, trees,
rocks, plants, animals, foods, medicines,
minerals, stories, and special places.

Connections to Country include cultural
practices, knowledge, songs, stories, and
art, as well as all people: past, present,
and future.

Ngadjuri, Peramangk, Kaurna Country:
Barossa Valley region
South Australia

Dedicated to Bianca:
live freely live fiercely

Published by Centred in Choice
https://centredinchoice.com
PO Box 448 Alice Springs
Northern Territory 0871 Australia

about the author

Heather Anne Gordon is a writer
based in South Australia whose work
flows between landscape and life.

This collection draws from twenty
five years of journals and lived
observation.

Heather's writing flows
unconventionally; part reflection, part
song, part fierce conversation with
the land and those who nurture it.

contents

acknowledging country

acknowledging
as well as respecting country

is acknowledging breath

the first inhale
of morning mist over water

the deep spirit thread
binding first peoples to land

to rivers that remember
to hills that speak

to the trees who hold song
the rocks who carry story

the land keeps their heartbeat alive

to animals who teach
patience and courage

to foods that sustain
and medicines that heal

to the megafauna
sleeping below the earth

to sacred places
pulsing with time itself

acknowledging
as well as respecting country

is honouring all of this

the ancient lines of song
drifting on wind

the stories that map stars
and seasons

the practices of care
that shape fire and soil

the art that traces belonging
in ochre and weave

knowledge
that has lived unbroken

through countless generations

it is recognising people
past present future

elders who keep the flame alive

children who learn to walk
in rhythm with country

those yet to come
who will inherit the gift

a gift of belonging
not owned but carried

shared through survival
through love through truth

acknowledging
as well as respecting

is also   remembering
the unfinished work of justice

the silences imposed
the dispossessions endured

the strength of custodianship
that resisted all erasure

the resilience that still flows
like underground water

always rising always returning

to speak these words
is not ritual alone

it is promise
it is commitment

to listen   to learn
to walk gently

to face the history
that lies beneath our feet

to understand
that this land has never been empty

that country holds us
if we choose to be held

that to acknowledge
as well as respect
is to live differently

to act with care and with courage

to lean into truth
that was always here

knobby club rush

knobby club rush gathers
in great green clumps

brown knobby seed heads
rising above the water

still pools cradle
its sheltering arms

a sometimes rowdy wetland
where small lives thrive

frogs sing from its tangled base
their foam nests clinging
like secrets in the reeds

tiny voices ripple
across the dusk

the rush holds it all
in patient grace

dianella revoluta the black anther lily
holds her blue star flowers like sparks
above the brown earth of the barossa
valley as barossa lily writes her life
not in splendour but in the pulse of
change and rain her words weaving
with outback lily fierce across the arid
plains and the andamooka lily flower
crinum luteolum rising with pale
blooms from sand dune and
subsistence together they murmur of
ordinary women and ordinary lives in
a southern land each voice rooted in
persistence each voice leaning toward
light even when the world is too busy
to notice

© Heather Anne Gordon: 2024 December

gratitude

how to explain to my supporters
that i am giving up all pretences
i am throwing away full stops
at the end of sentences
no capitalisation no punctuation
casting off the restrictions
of the government style guide
it is like
learning a new language
not useful perhaps
but necessary
for it is the way
i am writing down
what comes into my head

the first draft trembles raw
unfinished
breathing possibility and peril
to share it
is to risk being broken open
to confess courage and fear
in equal measure

early readers see me
unpolished
they sit with halting sentences
and broken lines
no pretences only the pulse
of story beneath the noise
they do not turn away
instead they call me forward

companionship is their gift
against the tides of doubt
that drag me under
they steady me
like a guide rope
stretched across a dark road
their patience becomes rhythm
their curiosity sparks fire
when mine burns low
they travel with me
to kitchen tables and campfires
to small town pubs
and quiet verandahs
to the digital glow
of online nights
listening to characters
and stories
not yet whole
this devotion
cannot be measured

in the barossa years
the vineyards
held their breath in winter frost
rows of vines sleeping
while my own blood
thickened and slowed
the air heavy with mist
pressing down on valley floors
cellar doors alive with visitors
while i stayed home
with pain

yet friends came
bringing soup and stories
we sat at the kitchen table
crowded with crockery
and laughter
they helped me see
past the cold
into the slow patient rhythm
of vines

they asked questions
that carried me through
the silence
they believed
when i could not

in the andamooka years
the sun and sky remade me
mullock heaps crouched
like discarded dreams
around the town
mulga trees scratching
the endless sky
dwellings of tin and rock
weathered by decades of wind
the arid zone
stripped away pretence
stone and silence
forced me to listen differently

friends
still walked beside me
even from afar
their companionship
bridged the wide dry spaces
their contact steadied me
when i felt lost
among empty diggings
their laughter reached me
across the flat horizon
reminding me
i was not alone in that vastness
on sala days
they came to see
what i had gathered
paintings and words
strung together like survival

their presence
turned bare walls
into celebration
sometimes
my friends entered
the stories themselves
their gestures their names
their voices their kindness
threaded
into the worlds i built
many diversions many paths
many memories
i could not always remember
why i began

not every suggestion
found its way onto the page
some i turned aside
choosing rebellion
over certainty
trusting the story to unfold
in its own time
even refusal
became part of the making

every draft   every episode
every scene
is stitched with invisible threads
of friendship
criticism offered as care
encouragement as survival

voices that told me
when pain stole the day
when illness took more
than i wanted to give

to publish is not arrival
but surrender
to lay down words
as both humility and courage
these stories are mine
but never only mine
they bear the fingerprints
of all who touched them
those who asked
the hard questions
those who stayed
through the silences
those who believed
a voice like mine
was worth hearing

i want these stories to ring true
not as echo but as imprint
each sentence pressed
with the presence of others
and when i fling these words
into the world
they carry not only my voice
but the chorus of many

to my friends
during the barossa
and andamooka years
to those who visited me
through vineyards in mist
and the arid zone
who cheered me online
when my confidence faltered
who listened
when the words
were not yet whole
i relate these episodes
for without you
there would be no book
no offering
only fragments left unheard

for this chorus
i am grateful

© Heather Anne Gordon: 2025 August 6

bread

writing bakes like bread

a process of lone creation

share to warm the heart

© Heather Anne Gordon: 2025 April 13

dragons

when i first moved
to the barossa

cassie

my sydney son's dog
lived with me

one early morning
she growled deep

then full bark
then bolted outside

fierce as the wind

and through her barking
i heard it

a heavy huffing breathing thing

still in my pjs
i stepped onto the back porch

no sheltering verandah
back then

and there it was

a basket hovering
directly over my back garden

people staring down

flames leaping from the basket

whuffing into a giant balloon

i told cassie
it was only a dragon breathing

nothing to fear

and in the cooler months
the dragons returned often

we would hear their slow
patient breath above us

cassie would growl
to let me know
they had come home

but she no longer barked
at them

as if she too understood
their strange sky bound ways

one long weekend
the three day
balloon festival came

i was minding joy's dog

there were twenty two
dragons in the sky
each morning

and idgie barked and leaped
at every one

her body electric
each time the fire
burst into their bellies

this morning i lay curled in bed

the air thick
with a frantic breath

that dragon is in trouble
i told myself

so i shuffled out the front
in my pjs again

and there it was

huffing awkwardly

low and unsteady

between the houses behind
nuriootpa retirement living

i scuffled
to the poultry palace
for a better view

lifted my camera

caught the shimmer of its body

and without realising

caught the tiara
on the poultry palace too

stepped onto the road
for another shot

but the growl
of a four-wheel drive
forced me back

the support crew had come

faces turned to the sky
searching
for their wandering beast

they were a little lost

rain began to spit on my face

the air smelled of wet dust
and cooling flame

a faint hiss
from the great nylon skin
as it sagged

i went inside

switched the heater on

sat at the computer

took a few more photos
through the window

and then watched
as the dragon folded in on itself

its fire gone

its breath quiet

settling into the wet earth

with the long slow sigh
of an old friend

and i thought
of cassie and idgie

how they would have
danced and barked

and told me all about this one

how silent the house has been
without them

yeah nah blah blah

the aussie chorus line
half promise half shrug

a dance of words
where meaning slides off

like sunscreen in the heat

a tiara for the poultry palace

tom turned up without warning

rachel trailing him
grinning already at the secret

he hauled from the ute
a welded arch with sharp points

i could not guess its destiny

rachel burst into laughter

tom steered us
straight to the chook house

that little cage
guarding hens from foxes

and sly cats through the night

sitting in the front yard
because
barossa nanna declared

the chooks
must be centre stage

scratching
soursob bulbs up to the sun

pecking joyfully

these were no ordinary chooks

they were the newly adored
ora family

beyond
barossa nanna and the lonely chook
book

sheila eva and stella
with their chosen names

woven from real lives

but the new brood
came simpler just as playful

aurora dora eudora
pandora torah

the ora family
clucking in harmony

tom lifted the curved metal
over the centre barrel

perfect fit he said
having measured in secret
last visit

*get some blue glass bottles
from the stash you are saving
for bottle screens* he ordered

so we did and there it rose

a blue tiara gleaming
for the poultry palace

the cage transformed
into splendour

no longer just safety
but royalty for hens

i was thrilled
crowing with delight

and later when meg came
she stared

puzzled by the glittering arch

what is that she asked

a tiara on a poultry palace
i replied

doesn't everyone have one

© Heather Anne Gordon: 2014 June 28

decluttering

decluttering feels like
sifting through memory dust

what to hold what to release
into another life

each object humming
with the weight of goodbye

© Heather Anne Gordon: 2020 August

corellas

corellas arrive from the sky
like raucous laughter

thousands of them
a rolling white tide

they circle the vines
with a shriek
that could split the dawn

the frosty air becomes foam
under their wings

a restless tide of feathers
and noise

i sit in the car
watching   wondering

why so much fuss
why this endless clamour

their voices rise
in a chorus unrefined

as if the only language
they know is

are you here are you here
are you here at last

their home the honeycomb cliffs

along the river at swan reach

yet the barossa vineyards
call them across

the gas guns thunder all day
in futile defiance

still the corellas
serrate gum leaves

flail supple branches

scratch their own small itches
with gleeful disdain

they feast on grubs
in the soil between the vines

their white bodies vivid
against the rich brown earth

pecking and clawing the dirt
with relentless delight

the air trembles
with the sound of their joy

some hang upside down
claws curled like questions

their wings wide their eyes lit
by private jokes

a brief yellow crest flashes
bright as flame

i wonder what each bird thinks
in that instant

what life means beyond
the scream and the play

at dusk they gather in trees

a nightly roll call of survival

who is here who has flown
who is missing
who is still alive

then the chorus softens
cuddle close now

against the deep silence
of dark   and quiet

they are seasonal tourists

visitors we love and curse
in equal breath

for we tore away their habitat

and gave them vineyards
instead

a banquet
never meant for them

yet they feast and remind us

that wildness
always finds a way

© Heather Anne Gordon: 2024 July

eldest daughter

from the muted sunrise
of her birth

she carries a legacy
of ancient scars

receiving trauma and grief

while smoothing
emotional reservoirs

parenting
while she is a sibling

a people-pleaser
the go-to sister for listening

burden and benevolence
weighing her heart

after too many years
she is walking away

making a new start

antidote

this disease moves through me

like wildfire through dry grass

my mind my body
stripped raw aching for relief

and so i answer with travel
with flights across the continent

silver wings carrying me
to friends   carrying me to colour

each departure a small rebellion
against despair

first sydney then canberra thursday
twenty seven
september to monday night
the first of october
with tony aark

for floriade
how fabulous is floriade

flowers spilling their secrets
across commonwealth park

layne beachley
opening the gates of spring

icons legends myths
blooming in beds of tulips

then back at work on tuesday

but wednesday
i claim for myself
a day of recreation leave

to walk among grassy woodland

within cromer conservation park

learning the names
of native grasses

their whispers in the wind

rooted in soil older than sorrow

thursday back at work again

despite being instructed

to use all my rec leave
before december

so friday afternoon
the road calls me west

to elliston for siv's birthday
on the twelfth

a stop in wilmington
to see tess and jim

a sunday in the barossa

wrapping me back into home

the week of fifteen through
nineteen october back at work

but saturday twenty through saturday
twenty seven

i fly north to broome

where pindan soil
meets turquoise sea

and the horizon holds me
in its endless embrace

you ask does this cost money

of course it does

but money is the balm
for what the body cannot mend

each ticket a salve each journey
an antidote

against the disease
that ravages mind and bone

against the silence that waits
if i do not move

travel is my consolation
my medicine my relief

each mile a refusal
each reunion a healing

across australia
i scatter myself like petals

returning not cured
but alive still alive

fading blinds and fading minds

cognitive strength fades
with time when senses

lack their joyful rhyme
beige   dull spaces

a silent crime   interiors
with our thoughts confine

making minds wither
past their prime
fading curtains

drab and worn
in greige interiors
our minds are torn
stimulus wanes

creativity is scorned
in such dull settings
thoughts forlorn
where vibrant ideas
are seldom born

in rooms so beige
our senses sleep
emotions dulled

thoughts not deep
a canvas blank
our minds to keep

no vibrant colours
through windows peep
inspiration   struggles to leap
bright hues and art   invite

stimulate senses
minds ignite
curtains vibrant

rooms alight   spaces
where ideas take flight

in colourful settings
we thrive in the light

mosaic magic

november two thousand eleven
i remember the glow

a gallery filled with light
and art and laughter

thylacines circling
a great round sphere

hands pressed against mirror
eyes wide in wonder

as if my hands gave shape
to what the world
had already lost

the architect
and the printmaker drifted in

their footsteps echoing
like quiet blessings

they carried the ball
to the town of robe

a treasure resting by the sea

and i felt the shimmer
of destiny in their gaze

the pink mermaid egg slipped
from my hands to another's

carried away
for hundreds of notes

somewhere it whispers luck
into the corner of a home

her sister found castlemaine

where voices of craft
and memory are alive
in the gardens

a floral ball burst into bloom
in april

its petals and mirrors
now radiant in perth

a piece of me scattered
across the continent

threaded through landscapes
of sand sea and eucalyptus air

my work breathing
in distant rooms

i posted on social media then
because
excitement demanded it

i bragged not for glory
but for proof of survival

my mosaics leaping
from table to pedestal to heart

each sale a reminder
that magic existed

even when my body
trembled with betrayal

for the disease
came stealthy and unkind

ravaging marrow and mind
with hidden teeth

methotrexate
my cruel companion

offering reprieve with one hand

and stealing radiance
with the other

yet still
i laid down crockery shards
like devotions

colour beside colour
a rhythm that steadied me

each fragment a fragment
of pain turned jewel

each curve of tile
a small defiance
against the genes
woven into my immune system

i never thought myself an artist

only a woman gathering pieces

making sense of fracture
by seeing it differently

until one day i woke and knew

this was the way i meditated

so let me tell you
of mosaics and illness
intertwined

of eggs
that sang mermaid songs
across states

of thylacines that danced
in galleries

of medicine that burned
but could not kill

the spark that let me
belong
in the world of art

© Heather Anne Gordon: 2012: September

motivational chat to myself

dawn

hear the magpies warble

add sparkle to your life

let critics fuel the flame

remember: this is not the end

© Heather Anne Gordon: 2025 May 28

sydney adventure

i land in sydney

thursday night

virgin blue wings
cutting through twilight

terminal two touchdown

got a plan got a list

adventure in my bones

can not resist

what have i missed

sydney son told me

next time
send your plan in advance

so i sharpened my pencil

this trip is not left to chance

three levels deep

star-marked hash tagged plus

with flex
for the locals i trust
no fuss

essential

cirque du soleil
flip the night into gold

that tuesday vibe
let acrobat dreams unfold

desirable

sunday paddle
around blues point

and berry bay stream

kayak under azure sky

like i am floating
through a dream

afternoon walk

berry island breeze

where the mangroves whisper

through gumtree leaves

art on tuesday
morning light spills bold

cazneaux frames stories

that never get old

working you ask

you bet i have jobs

from angel wings to hakeas
on hardwood floors

wolli pine is looking sad

repot and revive

then i am going ten rounds
with mould

and i will survive

but do not worry

i am here for more than plants
and grime

i have scheduled time with joy

i have curated time

joy is twenty years an aussie

since oh eight   oh eight
eighty eight

that is a party date fate

could not replicate

and anita

dialysis monday wednesday
friday tight

friendship finds rhythm
in the softest of light

we will talk between needles

and times the quiet steals

because visiting is not a maybe

it is a must that i feel

snakebean feeds me

quick thai food with spice

oxford street heat
with a side of rice

this whole street
has really got flair

serving fast-fused stories

in a neon glare

so do not tell me

this is not a plan that excites

it is a blueprint for wonder

mapped in late nights

i have pencilled in awe

and scribbled out stress

adventure is a contract

and i came to say *yes*

north sydney stand by

i am rolling with glee

a dash of the random

and full-hearted me

let us kayak let us laugh
let us artfully roam

for six sweet days

this wild town is home

© Heather Anne Gordon 2008
July 31 – August 6
1840hr thu 31 jul 2008 - 1910hr
wed 06 aug 2008

hospital hush

these are the rules
i carry with me

rule one no flowers no gifts

they do not belong
in this tidewater place

petals fall and scatter like foam

nurses cannot gather them

and i cannot hold them
against the current

let your kindness come
as light as rain on water

a thought carried downstream
not a weight in my arms

rule two no visitors unless i call

sometimes the body is an inlet
needing stillness

sometimes the spirit rests best
when alone

leave what i need at the shore
and let me drift

solitude becomes a gentle tide
pulling me inward

silence rises and falls
like the sea breathing

rule three is my care
written in stone
smooth as river rock

tony aark holds the map
to my crossing

no machines to tether me
to the bank

when the current
has already carried me beyond

let me go with the river's flow

let me slip into the tide
unresisting

so this is my hospital hush

a river rhythm soft and steady

rules that ripple
not to bind but to free

if you float with them
i will be cradled

if you follow their tide
i will be at peace

© Heather Anne Gordon: 2012: October 12

bienenstich

daria and i running to the gym each
noon subway in hand laughter on the
return she flew to tasmania leaving
me honey eaters on porcelain wings
six plates numbered fragile warning
of lead so i created a picnic mosaic
buzzing with bees deb's filigree plate
at the heart words along the edge
announcing *waiting for bienenstich
with daria* so she could see it at the
front door

the blonde mermaid

it was an outboard motor
that sealed the deal

that tom and i
are actually siblings

sharing d n a
across time
and tangled choices

i had begun mosaicing
the carport wall
with mermaids

in my head
there were always mermaids

i had only managed
a swirling fantasy rock

a place for her to lean or loll
or simply rest

she was alive in me
but not yet alive on the wall

tom and jenny came to visit

i had been discouraging visitors

i was self-medicating
for pain
and drifting in bad decisions

but tom wanted to see
what i was doing

so i shuffled down the ramp

showed him the fantasy rock

mirror and tile and stone
swirled together

i told tom about the mermaid

he pulled a construction pencil
from his top pocket

sketched her   lola
straight onto the wall

her arms thin her lips puffy
her buttocks defined

she sprawled against the rock
skeletal in outline

but i knew she would grow solid

once she was dressed in tile

then tom asked
about the daikin airconditioner

jutting ugly from the wall

every visitor had asked
the same question

and i gave tom
the same answer

*i am going to make it
into a daikin outboard motor*

tom understood at once
he demanded a long ruler

and with steady lines
drew the planks
of a wooden boat

no one else
had grasped this vision not one

he sketched the propellor
beneath the hull
and jenny pressed a tile

ceremoniously
into the centre of the propellor

anchoring it to the dream

giving me something true
to aim for

we had another coffee
then they left for home

i slipped back to bed

because visitors are tiring

even when helpful

even when they bring
mermaids into being

© Heather Anne Gordon: 2010 August

art

art must breathe and move
among us

not locked behind walls
or velvet ropes

galleries that whisper
only to the few

we need laughter scissors
colour and glue

let us make art social
let it spill into streets

parks kitchens classrooms
every hand joining in

fun art we seek
art that invites and includes

stories unfurling
values shining like sunlight

through art we speak and listen

shared experiences
weaving new worlds

art asks questions opens doors
holds treasure

every creation a spark
a heartbeat a bridge

© Heather Anne Gordon: 2024 December

long before ships
with white sails
touched these shores

the land and sky
sang with many voices

each mob with their own words

for the winged ones
the furred ones
the ones that swim

each name a thread
binding people to place

there were no empty plains
no unused waters

handling the earth with care

rock dams cradled the rain

seeds fell to the ground
with the promise of bread

fires spoke in the language
of renewal

fresh green called
the kangaroo to return

canoes curved from living trees

nets held the shimmer
of the river

traps whispered to the eels
come this way

budj bim sang its old song
of food and community

then sails cut the horizon
and the claiming began

the names of other lands

wrapped around
our own creatures

words from across the seas
smothered the old tongues

fields were trampled

by hooves
that had never known this soil

the sacred stories scattered
like seed in a storm

yet still the old names
live in the breath of elders

still the fire knows where to run

still the net and the trap
remember their making

and the land waits for those
who walk gently

calling each being
by the name
it has always known

© Heather Anne Gordon: 2022 September

r u o k day

in isolation on r u o k day
i find my own rhythm

a kettle singing gently
reminds me i am cared for

the sun falls across the table
scattering gold

and i begin to piece together
scraps of colour

each page of a concertina book
folds open like a friend

images spark laughter
memories and dreams

i ask myself am i o k
and the answer is soft
but steady

yes because even here alone
creativity keeps me company

in isolation i pick up my phone

a friend's voice spills warmth
into the quiet room

we share stories small victories
silly jokes

the distance between us
shrinks with every word

i send an image of my collage
a burst of colour

they reply
with their own creation
a spark of joy

even kilometres apart
our laughter
threads through the air

and i remember
that reaching out
is its own kind of healing

and then i lose myself
in the flow
hands moving scissors glue
and paper
thoughts wandering to shapes
and colours and patterns
time disappears
the world outside falls away
there is only this moment
this creation

and a gentle sense
of being alive

© Heather Anne Gordon: 2020 September

curling into the cave

you are creative
it is time to be brave

do not hide away
do not curl into the cave of fear

to offer your work
is to stand bare in the storm

vulnerability is not weakness
it is the pulse of truth

art has power it is undeniable

what you speak
through brush or word or hand

is a language beyond language

it resounds in places unseen

someone waits quietly
for your vision

your creativity is a key
they have been reaching for

i whisper these words
to myself first

to remember why i began

to hold close the spark
that illness and doubt
cannot steal

in speaking to you
i am steadying
my own trembling

we walk together
across this uncertain ground

there is beauty
in community in connection

each reflection gathered
becomes a chorus

each small offering
threads us closer

so be brave
do not dim the flame

let your art shine
as it gives off that glow

whether in a gallery
or a screen lit late at night

whether one person
or many pause to see

what matters
is that your art is alive

passion rising
like breath through each line

your vision reaching hearts
and setting them alight

© Heather Anne Gordon: 2012 September

floriade

floriade canberra
two thousand and seven

aussie icons myths and legends

unfurling like petals

spring
breaking the grip of winter grey

tulips rising daffodils nodding

pansies grinning wide

the land exhales colour

first the ute i see it rusting

faithful in the farmyard corner

tray
no longer carrying
fence posts or hay

instead holding tulips
and pansies like a cradle

labour transformed
into tenderness

australia remade with blooms

and near it the dunny
proud and plain

long drop honest as the sun

a seat cut from wood
for generations

toilet bathroom
whatever you call it

it stands as memory a joke
a truth

gnomes wait nearby
small and stubborn

bright painted faces
guarding the beds

children schools communities

gifting them myths each year

gnomes become warriors
dreamers
footy players and queens

and still they grin
their secret knowing smiles

the fridge magnet icons
return again and again

blokey kangaroo bug spray
in hand

shrimps on the barbie

emu in cork hat and thongs

vegemite lawnmower ned kelly
surf lifesaver

a chorus of satire

where is the woman's song

where is the hills hoist
swinging sheets

like flags of domestic glory

and still the flowers
keep flowing

tulips red as memory
gold as promise

daffodils like trumpets
calling us forward

each bulb a small act of courage
rising through cold soil

reminding us
to keep blooming despite

the ute returns
rusted beauty filled with colour

the dunny returns
wooden seat
a legend carved in humour

the gnomes return
joyful odd and beloved

the fridge magnet returns
still blokey still incomplete

and all the while
the flowers rise
like breath like desire

organisers
weaving the festival
with patient hands

gophers for access

stalls for gathering
marquees for dreaming

the australia fair street organ
pumping out music

brass and timber meeting
the wind

notes spilling into the tulips
like another kind of blossom

i circle the park slowly

with freedom on my wheels
with blossoms in my chest

the land alive the people alive

floriade flowing myths laughter
satire truth

australia in spring
bursting again into colour

memories

i remember the days of wild abandon
stopped by police and set free with a
wink my laughter running ahead of
me calling up tony aark with a grin
thinking he would clap my back yet he
turned it into a sermon and still even
sermons could not blunt the divine
sunshine of sparkling shiraz drunk
too quickly of campfire mornings
drenched in sunbeams and possibility

road trips with heike windows down
hair streaming wild apple cider
bottles sitting on the dashboard white
wine chilled for kayaking her voice
reminding me of mischief empty
bottles hidden in the work bin so my
house guest did not see them

tony aark already the wise one
chiding margie and me for drinking
with more clarity than we held and
we doubled over in laughter at the
absurdity of it all hangovers tasting
almost sweet because they belonged
to the free

but hidden in the folds of this charm
the shadow came a cruel intruder
tearing thought from mind gnawing
bone from flesh scribbling pain across
my body

they give me methotrexate a word
that tastes like metal a promise
wrapped in poison it whispers of
relief yet brings me low makes me
ghostly in my own body friends
remember the old tales their laughter
spilling over but mine falters tony
aark still stern in memory as if
wisdom could hold me steady

methotrexate promises help delivers
hollow fatigue nausea stains the
morning light joy becomes a fragile
glass that shatters too easily so i
confess the brittle places the nights
when laughter is a mask and friday
mornings when i cannot rise except to
inject another cruel dose

still the parties shimmer still the
laughter echoes somewhere within
me bright and reckless woven against
the dark hush of nausea charmed life
glimmers flickers beside the cruel
dose my laughter rarer yet still it
comes like a campfire flame in a storm
and that is how i go on

© Heather Anne Gordon: 2012: September

dragonflies

by the reeds in the creek
near the bushgardens
they shimmer
like thoughts made visible
thin wings catching sunlight
turning it to music
they hover
where water breathes slow
over stones worn gentle with time
each dart a whisper of balance
between air and river and memory

© Heather Anne Gordon: 2005 December

collage

when the mind feels heavy
like wet cloth on the line

you can tear the edges
of old paper

and find a softer kind of time

cut and paste and layer slow

let the colours pull you

where they know
you need to go

andamooka anna says

*each scrap
has its own secret tune*

barossa nanna nods slowly

*like the sun
over a warm afternoon*

and andamooka nanna smiles

as the scissors glide

*this is how
we stitch together
the places inside*

no one asks for a perfect frame

no gold seal no famous name

just the quiet joy
of glue and card

making beauty

from the everyday

is never hard

each scrap a whisper
each image a clue

to a story that waits

for a voice like you

when you slide into flow
you forget the ache

and the world becomes
wide
for your heart to remake

collage is gentle
it asks only your hands

it is paper and scissors
and shifting sands

it recycles it reuses
it brings old life anew

it is a small bright lantern
to create a sky of blue

children see lions
where you see leaves

they spin their own tale
as the paper weaves

together
you count the clouds
and the trees

and talk about colours
as free as the breeze

andamooka anna
with her sideways grin

and barossa nanna
with her patience within

and andamooka nanna
with her truth-telling eyes

make art that sings
and lets the hidden truths arise

making art is a kindness
to the soul

a patchwork path
that makes you whole

collage tells you
there is no wrong

only the rhythm
of your own strong song

© Heather Anne Gordon: 2021 April

kangaroo

soft thuds of paws through vines
tails sweeping dust
mothers pausing mid-bound
ears tuned to secrets
the valley breathing with them

© Heather Anne Gordon: 2005 October

**driving on ngadjuri and
nukunu country**

jamestown

to

spalding

r m williams way

deb is driving

barbara's car

atomic rush red

rav four

hybrid edge

heather is in the front seat

bemoaning the landscape

crops ruined   frosted

blunt   bleak

two bold rabbits

sitting under a tree

brazenly in the sunlight

where they should not be

from the back seat

barbara's voice is sweet

two dear little bunnies

she gently repeats

heather cocks her right thumb

and forefinger   in a line

points   and shoots

shouts *bang! bang!*

in double time

i bluddy hate rabbits!

in the silence that follows

no one speaks

the art of becoming

it is my first art exhibition
i have wandered
through others before of course

i have stood quietly
in white walled rooms
a volunteer in the background
helping hang canvases
with measured care

i even once
collaborated with friends
a sculpture on the cliffs
at elliston
in the year two thousand
and four

but this is different
this is my own work
in a group show five years later
and i am swollen with pride
yet trembling inside

the walls are rich
with colour and form
so gorgeously beautifully
displayed

that my little corner
might slip unnoticed
and part of me is glad for that
for then the critics
may pass me by
and i will be safe in my shyness
yet here i am
raw open exposed

i watch the people
circulate at the loud launch
wine glasses flashing in the light
talking as if they know
oh i like this one says
but will you buy another asks
and slowly they drift
around the room

until they arrive at my wall
my photographs
of south australian landscapes
my contribution
to the south australian
living artists festival

a month long celebration
of visual expression

i look at my work
stretched on canvas
i remember the hours
spent deciding
what to print
what to display
what to risk

and i feel a glimmer
of belonging
have i found my tribe at last
do i have permission
to speak in images
and even stranger to be here
at all
for someone else pulled out
and photographs were needed
so by accident or serendipity
i stepped in

i try to look casual
beside my work
as if conversation comes easily
when a woman approaches
glances at my grid of images
precisely hung
and with a curl of her lip says
i could take photos like that

something flares in me
sudden   hot
and i turn toward her
my voice more calm
than i expected

but have you exhibited i ask

do you put yourself out there

she falters

i am astonished at myself
astonished
at the rebellion rising
astonished
at the joy
of standing firm

for once i did not shrink
for once i answered back
and in that small moment
i was artist enough

© Heather Anne Gordon: 2009 August

boobook

more pork more pork
calling for more pork
not the pork you eat
mournful   outside my window
smallest of owls
calling into the night for company

© Heather Anne Gordon: 2009 August

dream house

once i chased hope
down the sturt highway

between nuriootpa and gawler
cold nights working long hours

my body breaking
under illness and pills

money
slipping through my hands
like water

treats and trips

to soften the blow
of days
that felt too heavy

then a house appeared
like a promise
walls i imagined
already mine
in my mind i had already
moved the furniture into place
the chair by the window
catching first light

the table set for pleasant meals
the bed
where i would finally
rest without worry
shelves lined with books
whispering company

a home fully alive
inside my imagination

in that dream
the garden bloomed
before i turned the key
purple and white hardenbergia
climbing over fences
lavender by the gate
to greet me home
vegetables rising from rich soil
a sanctuary
planted against the ache
of the world

but debt
was waiting
quietly in the corner
credit cards swollen
no deposit to offer
tony aark came especially
from sydney

numbers laid bare
the truth i tried not to see
the furnished rooms of my mind
stood in stark contrast
to the bare emptiness of reality
a house beyond reach
walls hollow without me
dreams of fragrant
native frangipani
turned brittle like dead leaves
the garden in my head withered
before the first seed
could touch the earth

no house no keys no beginning
inside those walls
only tears and the ache
of disappointment
a week of sorrow
then the card declined
insufficient funds
a sharp voice of reality
teaching me that dreams
without ground
cannot root

so i turned to saving
step by step
tending to debt
like pulling weeds
from a crowded bed
learning that patience
is its own kind of harvest
hope planted deeper
than desire
for quick blossoms
nurtured slow in the soil
of self-discipline

and still i carry the vision
a garden that waits
beyond the debt
rooms already furnished
in my mind
light falling just so
across the floorboards
i never owned
a house that remains
a half-remembered promise
bitter with distance
sweet with longing
close enough
to touch in thought
yet always just out of reach
in life

© Heather Anne Gordon: 2008 August 6

from outback lily...

out here
where the gum trees sway
in this vast land where i stay
racism lurks   a quiet blight
casting shadows
stealing light

not just whispers
not just stares
it invades the health we bear
chronic stress   it takes its toll
on body   spirit   heart
and soul

from blood pressures
that start to climb
to immune systems
worn by time
the fires of inflammation blaze
and health declines
in subtle ways

our first nations face the strain
of prejudice
that feeds their pain
already at risk
their hearts endure
a weight too heavy   harsh
premature

sleep disrupted
nights of dread
dreams disturbed
by fears widespread
it is more than tiredness
it is a breach
into health
that these nights leech

weathering
steals the years away
premature aging on display
a storm inside
that doesn't cease
a quiet thief   denying peace

the immune system
battles strife
vulnerability sowed
by prejudice rife
each insult felt
each hateful jest
a verbal blow
that leaves the body
stressed

from strokes
to heart attacks so real
the costs of hate are wounds that heal
slow and heavy   if they mend
for hate gives harm that knows
no end

here in the bush
where stars ignite
dreaming of change
a future bright
where justice reigns
where all can thrive
and health is ours
kept alive

but to get there
we must see
racism's cost   its cruelty
not just a wound of the heart
or mind
but one the body knows
confined

together we must build a space
where all are cherished
every race
with first nations wisdom
standing tall
the oldest culture
a guide for all

barossa lily...

out here in the barossa sun
where vineyards stretch
and creeks run
racism hides in casual guise
in offhand jokes
and sideways eyes

it is not the shouts
or blatant jeers
but quiet words that sting
for years
a comment here
a glance askew
the kind of harm
that's hard to view

just a joke they often say
but jokes like these
do not fade away
they linger   heavy
in the air
a weight that's cruel
a weight unfair

stress builds up
it doesn't show
but deep inside
the damage grows
blood pressure spikes
the heart beats fast
the toll of prejudice
amassed

sleep disrupted
restless nights
dreams invaded by old slights

it is more than tiredness
it is a drain
a health decline
that leaves its stain

weathering
steals the years ahead
aging faster   spirits bled
the body bears
what words impart
a silent ache   a heavy heart

immune systems falter too
worn down by
what is lived through
each comment felt
each subtle slight
a battle fought
a constant fight

in this valley
where life seems sweet
casual racism taints the beat
it is in the shops   the pubs
the streets
in quiet whispers
on sculptures neat

so here i sit   i have seen it all
the way it builds
the way it falls
and i dream of change
a brighter day
where kindness blooms
and hate gives way

together
we must break the chain
of casual harm   of quiet pain
for health and peace
for all to thrive
let us build a world
where love is alive

© Heather Anne Gordon: 2025 April 9

abandoned

what lingers in the silence
of abandoned yards

the bush takes back
yet still shows scars

immigrant hands etched stories
into broken dreams

© Heather Anne Gordon: 2025 September

the shed

all day i have been haunted

by visions of a tidy shed

shelves whispering order

art supplies
holding future stories

in my mind
i weigh each token of chaos

deciding what lives
and what fades

then a glance at the clock

after four p m

the day sighs
too late to begin

© Heather Anne Gordon: 2025 April 27

magpie

morning song bird
black and white composer of dawn
notes flung like ribbons
across cold light
each warble a map of home

© Heather Anne Gordon: 2005 September

fogs and frost

i am tired of winter
with its fogs and frost

its chilly breath
tightening sinew and bone

each gust a command
to shrink to fold to hide

yet still i whisper let it rain

let it rain more than enough

for the earth is thirsting
and the rivers are dry

for all this talk of climate baking

still i must hold myself
curled against the cold

i am no creature of frost
no not me

i long for warmth
not scorching not cruel

just the soft kiss of sun
on bare skin

enough for life to flourish
enough for vitamin d

not the sear
that cracks flesh into cancer

but the languid evenings
where breath runs easy

where i can stretch
every inch of being

and feel the body alive at last

years in the barossa
taught me the vines love winter

but my veins thicken
my bones turn to stone

they said i would get used to it

they said
you can get used to anything

then why does the blast of heat
from bitumen

strike like revelation when i
step to the road

why does the scent of first rain
on parched ground

rise up and name my home

petrichor come and claim me

they came with ships with cages with
sacks of seed they came calling it
empty they came calling it theirs
despite letters patent but the land
already sang with story with law with
kin first nations held memory in soil
and stone in stars across the night sky
in songlines running deep as water
and wide as horizon

settlers did not listen they tore the
ground they split the silence they
brought cats with hunger rabbits
burrowing foxes stalking camels
trampling donkeys horses sheep
cattle grinding down fragile country
until dust storms rose red as rage
choking the breath of earth

and the cursed plants prickly pear
blackberry salvation jane soursobs
boxthorn olive tree each thorn each
root another invasion another
suffocation smothering native plants
strangling ancient gardens

burning out the food the medicine the
shelter that belonged

first nations grieved they watched
country groan they saw rivers shrink
and soil collapse but they carried
resistance in their bones they carried
remembrance in their songs they
remembered the night skies mapped
with ancestors they remembered the
hills marked by story they knew the
balance that was broken

and still they kept telling it still they
keep telling it

tourists clap at purple fields call it
wildflower gaze at golden soursobs
call it charm they do not know the
poison the death they do not hear the
silence where birds once sang they do
not feel the grief that lives in country

every hoof every claw every thorn is
conquest that never ended but still
first nations speak still they fight they
burn they heal they plant they hold
the memory of balance and they say
this wound is not forever they say
country can be mended with care
with respect with listening

machines came colonisers stayed
ferals multiplied but story never died
across the skies across the land
memory runs deeper than conquest
resistance runs fiercer than foxes
sharper than thorns first nations hold
it still

the land remembers it still

© Heather Anne Gordon: 2023 August

sleeping

long before our breath
could be heard

before the first fires
were coaxed into being

a shallow sea
lay across the heart of this land

its waters cold and endless

its skin broken
only by the rise
of ancient creatures

long necks slicing through blue

flippers carving the silence

turtles drifting slow as prayer

their bones sleeping now
in the dark earth

their shape reborn
in colours of fire

opal gleaming
in the quiet hands of miners

opal telling the story of seas
that no longer move

andamooka rests
on the rim
of that vanished shore

its dust whispering to the sky

that once it was salt and tide
and moonlight

beneath all this
the sandstone holds its gift

water older than cities

older than the first footsteps
on this soil

seeping through time
until it finds a way to the light

through the mound springs
where life gathers

birds lifting
from the green edges

people walking trade routes
older than memory

carrying the songs of water
across the desert

in the great artesian basin

that ocean is still there

it learned how to hide

losing my grip

the childproof cap surrendered

spinning from my fumbling hold

pill armies cascaded

like grey-green marbles
across the vinyl battlefield

i bent over the speckled storm

fingertips grazing each remedy

a gust of giggles caught me
off guard

hiccupping through the chaos

i looked up

throat still trembling with mirth

phone poised at the brink
of fame

shall i freeze this moment
of defeat

for the scrolling crowd's
applause

or their sneer

perhaps   somewhere

losing my grip could become

a quiet celebration
of my humanness

digital heartbeat

as i digitise more than fifty years of
print photos i move through
fragments of years each image a soft
ache of remembering your baby face
your first steps the sandpit the swing
the school portraits and further on a
whole life now glowing in screens of
light i reach for them as i once
reached for you and in every touch i
am asking did you ever know how
utterly i adored you

© Heather Anne Gordon: 2025 August

pink

tall self-sown shirley poppies sway
big fluffy doubles of soft pink
their faces open to bees
pollinators hum through warm air
the stems lean gentle in the breeze
fat seed pods
forming like bold promises
the soil rich from seasons of care
every petal a reminder
that love once planted
keeps returning

© Heather Anne Gordon: 2005 September

wongulla

at dawn
i drove from nuriootpa

leaving cloud and idgie
curled in the morning haze

my spirit surged
past mallee swathes

chasing promise
carved in brightening light

to walker's flat
the meeting place

a day of kayaking
from wongulla

my favourite place
i left comforts behind
and embraced the quest

reggie renault's engine hummed
beneath the rapidly rising sun

a steady grin curved
across my face

anticipating
a day on the water

then tom's caravan of laughter
rolled in

the kayaks hungry
for the river's call

fuelled by banter
and dawn's hum

we perched   poised
on adventure's threshold

hearts synced   to the pulse
of uncharted waters

beneath scattered clouds
we mapped our course

wongulla lagoon's mirror
glinted blue

we hauled our kayaks
beyond the sandy lip

plotting rendezvous
by smoky steel grills

awaiting sally

awaiting kym

no gilded comforts
just the wind's demand
and water's dare

beneath our clenched resolve
a boiling vault of grey
concealed ambush above

southerly whips
carved ice-scars on our cheeks

gone was yesterday's furnace

the blaze
replaced by keen breath
biting at our skin

determined individuals
braced for nature's revolt

we met cool defiance
with warm resolve

minds primed
for triumph

sidewinds howled
each paddle stroke
a duel with fate

we hunted shelter
where reeds murmured mercy

ignorance
guided nick's bold hands
as his kayak
pitched and bucked

its plastic hull
mocked
my camera's future dive

still we pressed on
through spray and challenge

our hearts

anchored
by sheer determination

we plunged
along the lagoon's inner seam

rain needles pricking
with wild invitation

then   wind once foe
turned ally

with a rebel's shove
hurling our keels
toward the river's
swirling current

rachel and tom
leading
in a borrowed double kayak

strength
woven between
each cautious breath

adventure
hailed us
at the murray's fast flow

sheer cliffs loomed
ancient cathedral walls

honeycombed stages
for cockatoo choirs

limestone veils
dripped warmth in toffee tones

a sea of rock
etched by eons' patient hand

a lonely gate
dangling on the vertical edge

a marker
of water's endless rise and fall

the cliffs stood sentinel
to our defiant passage

five hard kilometres
carved by paddle blades

a challenge
sculpted into the waking hours

i smiled
at limits honed
through sweat and banter

remembering richard's
joking
midnight jibe

about pressing
a week's worth of iron days
into one

yet here
fatigue tasted
of honest progress

adventure crowned
by weary triumphant limbs

nick emerged drenched
the river's trial   unfinished

tom steered us back
through defiant mirror-water

to his silent ute
to my reggie's waiting grin

nick rebirthed
in dry clothes and fizzy cheers

we christened his new toy
with yellow sparkling wine

paddles sang promise
on the kayak's rail

inspired hearts proving
nick's decision to kayak
telling tom
if she can i can too

flames cracked life
into aussie chops and snags

steel grills spun steaks
like daring dreams

sal's sushi jewels
brightened our wongulla feast

my brown bread and mussels
lent earthy might

mushrooms grapes and
rockmelon

danced colours
across the afternoon

a second bottle
of yellow sparkling
sealed our bond

then
nick slipped away
frightened by our fire

sal and kym plunged
down tumbling currents

tom and rachel
balanced on outrigger hopes

i steered my kayak
through chopping wake

the sky bled azure
among broken clouds

speedboats carved
encore wakes through our path

each crest endured
with fierce determination

our four kayaks
slicing through uncharted chaos

at the cliff's base
we sought a hidden inlet

but wind and wake
repelled our daring craft

twice our bow slanted
by a skimming speedboat

rain-slicked limestone
mocked every attempt

rachel's scream
cleaved the air
as a carp leapt

dark water
luring ghostly uneasy thoughts

we steeled our courage
against omen's call

undeterred
we charted the river's heartbeat

turning bows
toward where two waters marry

our paddles synced
in steely resolve
each stroke   a promise
to taste unmarked shores

the confluence beckoned
its dual currents pulsing

adventure surged
at the meeting's edge

we rose   unified
in that winding quest

our backs
kissed by tailwinds
a private cheer

yet rogue wakes
leapt to challenge our craft

rachel and tom   yielded
at the two hundred and twelve
kilometre mark

but sal
kym
and i
pressed toward the confluence

waves
bellowed revolt
kym's kayak
spun and sank
he surged ashore
chest wrapped by p f d
defiant

sal and i
wrestled the hull
triumph torn
from the storm

red wine glimmered
in the dying sunlight

tom and sal
poured courage
into my glass

i toasted safety
with equal measure of cheer
warning of water's hunger
when wine runs free

laughter rippled
over my cautious decree
their amusement jostled
like playful storm squalls

i stood firm
tempered
by the river's forge

© Heather Anne Gordon: 2007 March 11

borage

self sown and wild and tall
the feral bees all over it
drunk on blue stars of bloom
the leaves soft and edible
the stalks thick with tiny needles
beauty with boundaries
grace that stings a little
reminding me that even gentleness
knows how to defend itself

© Heather Anne Gordon: 2005 September

judging

we judge by what we see
in the moment

this shuffling breathless body

once swam and dived
once paddled rivers and lakes
washington and alexandrina

once white water rafted
the colorado river

and climbed mountains

camped under outback skies
for weeks at a time in my swag
identified and recorded the flora

a five state holiday
with two children and two dogs
no mobile phone
no g p s   paper maps

rescued a woman
from a burning house

travelled alone in the arid zone

the inner strength
unseen   still flows
only writing remains

© Heather Anne Gordon: 2025 October 6

bush turkey

once we were many
across the red earth

our feathers woven
into the dreaming

our steps
part of the old songlines

our nests built
only when the rain was kind

our children few
so the land could breathe

we kept the balance
of grass and wing and claw

when grasshoppers
came in their raging tide

we gathered from far and wide
and feasted
until the green returned

until the silence of chewing
was broken by new growth

then ships came
and with them
teeth and hooves
that never slept

guns that took us for sport

hands that cleared
our feeding grounds

for hungry flocks
of another kind

we were driven
into corners of the country

names like turkey flat
carved from the bones
of our gathering places

now in the memory
of most who walk these streets

when they say turkey
they do not see us

they see
the broad breasted stranger

from across the seas

a bird whose image
rides on the back
of hollywood films
on supermarket shelves
in the false snow
of christmas cards
and a rite called thanksgiving

we are written out of the feast
out of the language
of celebration

our name taken
our image replaced

as the american bird
struts through
the australian kitchen

its body sold as tradition
its story told
as if it belonged here

still in the quiet places
we remain
under the slow heat of the sun

scratching for beetles
in the sand

waiting for the time
when our own name

will be spoken again
without the shadow
of another upon it

© Heather Anne Gordon: 2022 April

ravens

aark aark they call across paddocks
black shimmer of thought on the wind
not crows but ravens
old storytellers sharp eyes
catching everything we miss
their voices
echo wisdom and mischief both

© Heather Anne Gordon: 2005 February

native currants
once grew thick across the land

german settlers
gathered them in the bush

family picnics
long days of berry picking
turned into dark tart jam

for a long time the custom held
yet some grew restless
with the prickly branches

pulling whole roots
to claim the fruit more quickly

possums once feasted
on the berries

emus carried the seeds
inside their journeys

these scats played their part
in scattering life

© Heather Anne Gordon: 2016 March

writing

you may wonder
why i even want to publish
these scraps from my blog

this ordinary life
scattered across hours
across years

as though anyone might care
and yet i return again and again

because i want
my granddaughter to know

not necessarily
the hidden rooms of my heart

but the shapes of the days
the choices made and unmade
the refusals
that made me determined

someone wiser tells me

please note poetry is

generally

not commercially viable

and i smile

because it was never
about the marketplace

it was about story

about a voice moving
across a generation

so she will remember me
as one who wrote

not as one
who sat blank
before the pokies
feeding coins
to their endless hunger
like so many i see

i think of all the things
i am not doing

all the ways i am not lost

because i am here

writing

wallaby grass

soft tufts dancing in dry wind silver
seed heads shimmer like memory
roots deep in patient soil holding the
hillside through every season quiet
hero of the valley floor

the bike shelter

tom had been working
long hours and long days

long years
in the construction industry

then suddenly
his employer went bust

tom out of work out of money

julia gillard's
fair entitlement guarantee

bought him time
though the thirty two pages
of feg paperwork
were daunting at first

he brought it all to my house
and my computer
he said his fat fingers
could not hit the right keys

apparently mine could

so many people fighting
for so few jobs

tom filled some of his days
at my house

we called each project
by the day of the week

a tuesday project was born
a bottle screen to hide the bins
and a massive bike shelter
built over an old hills hoist
clothes line

we gathered bicycle wheels
and frames

all donated for the cause
to fill the space

where a great callistemon
had once stood

until a sudden wild cold
southwest wind change

after days of fierce hot
northerlies

split the tree apart

two days before
my open garden

neighbours rallied
to carry off the branches

i placed a small sign
under an umbrella
for the visitors

to remind gardeners
that not all goes to plan

and nature is the real boss

tom sweated and swore
and built the shelter

i planted a deciduous creeper

parthenocissus tricuspidate
to soften the metal

joolz' son's monsoon bike
wired into the back wall

casey and stu delivered
a ute load of bicycles

tom's grandson tyson
donated his little bike

jaybee's cousin sharon's big red
with basket and light
the crowning glory

when it was done
tom and i drove to roseworthy

metal scraps
piled in the back of the ute

traded for a few notes and coins

just enough for wild turkey
and smokes

© Heather Anne Gordon: 2015 January

post-menopause moodiness

anger coils beneath my skin

counting hours
counting wages never paid

measured by moods
by mascara

by the width of my waist

told to shrink   to swell
to shush   to please

shamed for silence   punished
for speaking

holding my emotions   within
you demand my smile

would it kill me   yes   yes
it would

© Heather Anne Gordon: 2025 July 13

tadpoles

small commas of life in still water tails
flicking like questions to the moon
they breathe stories of becoming from
silence to croak to song the promise
of rain made visible

© Heather Anne Gordon: 2009 November

mermaid meditation

close your eyes

we will count the tide together

inhale slowly

one   two   three   four

the water rises

warm around your fins

you feel the soft pull of the tide

the hum of the noise outside

becomes the thrum of the deep

exhale slowly

one   two   three   four

release the shore

let it drift away

your body is lighter now

the current cradles you

as a mother holds her child

inhale slowly

one   two   three   four

see the mermaids

of the cold northern seas

their hair silvered with salt

their songs curling through fog

they have watched ships

since the first oars

touched water

exhale slowly

one   two   three   four

you pass them with a nod

they smile knowing

you are on a gentle voyage

they open the way for you

to go deeper

inhale slowly

one   two   three   four

now

the brown mermaids appear

in the cool shadow of pandanus

their bronze scales glimmer

in the dappled light

their eyes hold the history

of every stream and billabong

exhale slowly

one   two   three   four

they bless the water for you

they promise

safe passage

through the unknown

the flood will not come today

only the soft rain of peace

inhale slowly

one   two   three   four

you float with them

in still water

your heart steady

your mind quiet

the air fills you

as the tide fills the bay

exhale slowly

one   two   three   four

you are here now

held in the deep calm

each breath a gentle wave

each gentle wave a promise

you are safe

you are supported

you are home

keep breathing

© Heather Anne Gordon: 2021 November 13

bettong

once the night was alive
with small quiet feet

soft fur brushing the grasses

eyes like deep water
catching starlight

tails curled around
the green they gathered

returning to the nests
they shaped with patient care

they tilled the country
with no plough and no blade

turning earth
so the rain could sink

making cups for seeds to rest in

bringing life
up through the soil into the air

feeding the ones who grazed
and the ones who hunted

but the fox came
with its red hunger

the rabbit came
with its endless teeth

the sheep came
with its grinding mouth

the cat came
with its silent death

and behind them   men
who counted our bodies

by the dozen

sold for sport
on a sunday afternoon

bettongia pencillata

the name a whisper now
in this place

gone from the hills
and the valleys

gone from the shadow
of the gum trees

gone from the memory
of those who walk the night

without them
the soil lies hard and unbroken

the seeds wait
too long for the rain

the air grows thick
without the green to cleanse it

and the country forgets
the soft language

that once passed between earth
and small gentle paws

still in some places
far from here

they hop beneath the moon

they turn the soil
as they always have

holding in their digging
the memory of balance

the possibility of return

© Heather Anne Gordon: 2016 August

carobs

carob trees stand
patient in the barossa sun

roots deep in poor soil
still they give shade freely

their pods once ground
for sweetness in hard times

leaves holding green
when summers burn dry

heritage of hunger and comfort
living side by side

© Heather Anne Gordon: 2019 August

versing vs cursing

never ask
what my verses mean
feel the emotions they convene

let your mind wander
let it be free
interpret the words as you see

writers weave   secrets
playful and keen
imaginary thoughts
both intense and serene

share your thoughts   with me
if they bring glee

© Heather Anne Gordon: 2025 July 7

gayle

activist justice seeker defender of first
nations rights carer and worker
mother wife friend and media star her
voice steady as country wind her fire
never dimmed by struggle each word
a bridge each action a seed she stands
where truth needs standing and the
world grows fairer in her light so i
gave her the mosaic justice ball black
and white with yellow blossom and
blue sky

© Heather Anne Gordon: 2020 January

little brother creations

my brother tom and i
had a grand plan

to kayak
along the full length
of the river murray
in south australia

not all at once

he had too much work
and i had too little stamina

so we plotted it in sections

i scouted the river
during the week

marked possible launch sites

on the murray river pilot
by baker-reschke

a day here a day there

sometimes a crowd came along

sometimes just me and tom

and the one he called
his favourite niece
cloud the perfect dog

i hold close a photo of cloud
and tom

cloud perched like a captain
on the bow

tom paddling at big bend

the honeycomb cliffs
rising behind them

anzac day morning

tom's coffees fortified
with rum after the dawn service

he was in high spirits

telling stories
that had us laughing
as hard as we paddled

in the beginning
he borrowed my spare kayak

until joy
sold her two-person boat
bright yellow
tom managed it alone with ease

he named it skippy
for the way
it bounced on the water
later he added outriggers

before that
margaret joined us one day
we paddled from swan reach
to blanchetown

tom kept the commentary going
all the way upstream

sometimes to himself
sometimes to cloud

another time from blanchetown
to murtho and back again

dodging the waves
of speeding boats
their drivers
pretending ignorance
tom heckling them
about the speed limits
near kayaks

blanchetown became
our headquarters for a while

tom was working on the fishway
at lock one

after work it was easy
to slip onto the river

to watch the progress
at the lock

to walk behind
the tall sheets of steel
that held the water back

we kayaked
from wellington
to lake alexandrina

laughed our way through
the sheep dog trials

pretending to be judges

awarding every dog
perfect marks for effort
knowing we had the perfect
cloud

another day
we launched
from snowden's beach

skirted the wrecks
of the ship's graveyard
on the port river
yerta bulti

passed the old dynamite depot
across from the salt works

we swore
we would reach st kilda
by tea time

but the wind rose
quick and mean

cloud burrowed
·into the nose of my kayak
for cover

i fought the chop alone

until tom
clipped on a line
and towed us in

laughing
that cloud
looked braver than me

and he was right

one trip from morgan to cadell
felt different

i saw the old mortuary
near the ferry

and the skeleton
of a steam boat
against the bank

they planted seeds for a novel

the river feeding
both our paddling
and my writing

once tom and i inspected
a houseboat at a marina

i imagined it for my retirement

he crawled
through every corner

checked wiring water tanks
plumbing floats

but in the end we laughed

knowing it would never be
practical
for me

wongulla though wongulla

wongulla was always
my favourite stretch

wide and beautiful
i still dream
of those mornings there

at clayton bay
tom took us out in his boat
called wets end

his daughters horrified
when water seeped
up through the floorboards

tom grinning
said he was hoping
for a glass bottomed boat

then telling us all
to grab bait buckets
start bailing

from goolwa
he took joy and me
to tauwitchere barrage
and back

a mob of emus
waded in a line
through the shallows

tom said he had invited them
as our welcoming committee

another time from mannum

we went to younghusband

i showed off my boat licence
had it since the seventies

i steered
just long enough for tom
to lean back with a beer

he insisted
i wear his skipper hat
the one sarah
brought back from italy
he saluted me with a grin

sometimes
jenny drove the back up car

so long as
her phone battery lasted

once on the onkaparinga
her battery was flat

dark closing in

the wind against us

i was spooked
by the electricity pylons

marching across the water
in the dusk

tom laughed
called them drunken soldiers

he had been one himself

each stroke
against the headwind
a mix of comedy
and exhaustion

we laughed our way home
anyway

tom enjoyed
my open gardens
and open studios

he welded garden sculptures

he had always been creative

back in high school
he forged a candlestick holder
steel twisted into beauty
with copper

it still sits on the mantelpiece
he installed here

that candlestick
has lived in every house
i have lived in

at this house
tom built bottle screens

steel and glass sculptures
signed *little brother creations*

a name
that made us both laugh

tom died in the covid years

i could not be there
at the funeral

but as richard
joined the live stream
from overseas

i felt love still moving
as strong as the river current
as deep as the bond between us

from the fourth of february
nineteen fifty-six

to the thirtieth of june
twenty twenty

© Heather Anne Gordon: 2020 July 17

yertalla-ngga (flooding land)

hoffnungsthal
valley of hope
they called it then

peramangk
spoke of flooding land
again and again

the settlers
built their homes
upon a thirsty ground

but spring rains came
and the waters rose round

dreams were broken
where warnings were drowned

now hoffnungsthal
lies in a silence deep

a mirror of sky
where memories sleep

a place of still breath
of sorrow and grace

hard to imagine
the storm in this place

yet all its stories
linger and keep

© Heather Anne Gordon: 2000 May

the foot soak saga

hip replacement
at christmas
and a foot soak saga

managing solo
trying
to avoid the drama

walking with the frame
making it through

physio is on the way
tania's got my back
it is true

desperate
to soak my feet
cannot
wear shoes

cannot
bend down
i am stuck in the blues

dragged out
the big bowl
got it on the floor

filled it with water
both feet soaking
everything is sore

scrubbed
my left foot
feeling kind of cocky

right foot
is sitting on the edge
making the bowl a bit rocky

half an hour later
magazine   sponge and soap
on the table

magazine tips a bit
means
my phone is unstable

splash

my phone
hits the water   my heart
skips a beat

grabbed it out
quickly
like an athlete

turn it off
take the battery out
wipe it all down
no time to pout

careful

a slow journey
to the computer
do not want to slip
checked
the blackberry support site

it is a confusing trip
common theme
put the parts in rice

i have brown
not white
hope it will suffice

next morning

my hip
is burning
in pain
from yesterday's event

just sorting out the phone
left me feeling spent

but i am pushing through
got to stay strong

rehab is tough
but i keep moving along

© Heather Anne Gordon 2012 December 28

lisa

lisa carries songs easily
like pretty river stones
smooth and bright
her voice
gathers strangers
into circles of flame
winter nights soften
when she leans into melody
she walks roads unhurried
yet always arriving home
every fire becomes hers
when the music begins

© Heather Anne Gordon 2014 September 11 - 14

engaging my rage

engaging my rage
on my social feeds
venting my feelings
where unlikely anyone reads
words of fire emotions ablaze
posting my feelings
in this virtual maze
finding my voice
no longer concealed
in the digital world
my truth is revealed
donating to *destroy the joint* soothes
some needs

© Heather Anne Gordon 2024 November 23

the blue tree project oh sure yes the
intent is good yes yes we all clap our
hands and say awareness awareness
but blue paint on dead wood does not
build homes does not put food on
tables does not end family violence
does not reform courts does not pay
rent or wages or keep the fridge cold
and full it does not end the drug war
or fix broken systems and yet here we
are choking our own landscape with
toxins and glossing it over with the
colour of despair

they say the trees are dead but they
are not they are homes they are
hollows they are the hushed
chambers where birds nest bats curl
bugs crawl ants eat and fungi weave
their slow magic they are not dead
they are alive in another way habitat
in silver bark and soft grey and we
paint them blue and call it healing

but what is healing about poison
when it burns when it chips when it
flakes into soil and water what is
healing when a hollow once sanctuary
becomes a billboard a spectacle an
eyesore a jarring advertisement you
cannot look away from because
someone else decided you must look

slacktivism yes corporate marketing
genius yes breweries lotto sponsors
the irony the cruelty alcohol and
gambling as if they have ever soothed
the ache in the mind as if they do not
carve deeper wounds meanwhile the
companies clap themselves on the
back no wage rise no secure hours no
safety nets but a blue tree out on the
highway and somehow that is meant
to make us feel cared for somehow
that is meant to be enough

what about the men's sheds what
about the sporting clubs what about
the hundreds of dollars that could
fund mental health first aid training
instead of buying paint and brushes
what about the local services running
on scraps and breath that could use
that energy that time to actually hold
someone's hand through a crisis what
about funding counselling sessions
what about lowering the cost of living
what about fair work that does not
grind people into illness

it makes me furious that the silver
ghost of a tree once beautiful in its
starkness is drowned in gaudy blue
we are forced to look forced to accept
forced to pretend it means something
more than nothing when in truth it is
a billboard to grief but not to change a
loud scream of colour with no shelter
no bread no roof no justice nature
itself heals but painting over nature
with marketing does not

i know i know the origin was grief
was suicide was loss unbearable and i
do not diminish that i honour that but
i also know that this project is not the
way i would rather we let nature be
natural let the tree stand in its silver
skin quiet in its dignity and put our
money our time our grief our rage
into real change into jobs into safety
into care into each other because blue
trees will not save us they only cover
over what we do not want to face

zoo animals for kate

sam calls me over
to help bend metal into beasts
i mark lines in black
across the silver skin
his nibbler bites bright sparks
flying like helpless laughter
a silver sheet leaps wild
striking my head mid work
sam just grins says
get on with it and i do

a view from a far

debbie and i
bent over shards of crockery
and tile

our hands searching
for patterns in broken light

groundworks rising
from fragments
on the kitchen table

a language of colour
a river of patient glue

each piece
whispering
its place in the whole

then tony aark called
from the long dark road
between towns

his voice threading
into our circle of making

we told him of stories
hidden inside the mosaic

he named it *a view from a far*
like wings returning home

debbie's design unfolding
as landscape seen from air

© Heather Anne Gordon: 2013 May

out on the edge
of the ancient eromanga sea
vehicles squat in rusting repose

their damaged bodies
shot through with bullet holes

rare squares of skin
taken as trophies

to recreate as flora
from the arid zone

cleansing the land
and replenishing the waterholes

warm rain arrives
from the north west

on the last legs
of an ancient track

across an ancient land

on an ancient timeline
observed only by an emu
in the night sky

ephemeral flowers
sprawl across the landscape

their sensuous shapes
tempting tourists
who drive over ancient artefacts
unknowingly   ignorantly

out at the town dump
discarded cars and a bus squat
their bodies ready for recycling
mechanical tools bite and grab
tearing a test strip
creating another scar
searching
for a different coloured car

back in the metal workshop
the cutting and grinding begins
welding sparks arc
across the floor

the mask
and the welding gear
renders the worker
anonymous   deliberately

the artist
readies her paints
seeks the sensuous colours
of the flora

lovingly renders
the voluptuous flowers
on to the canvas
revelling in the shapes
and forms of the native flora

enchanted
by the seasonal offerings
of her adopted homeland
acquired by following her love
across the ocean

painting doesn't diminish
her loss
it allows a few hours
respite

aching with grief
she washes her brushes
excruciatingly   tenderly

the photographer
silently observes the interaction
between the welder the artist
and their subjects

envies their focus
their concentration

the meditation of the process
their talent

their ability to retreat
from the world
quietly   resentfully

we are all ephemeral

transitory   temporary

© *Heather Anne Gordon: 2023 May*

sparkling syrah

sparkling syrah in the glass

tiny stars rising to the rim

a bright fizz on the tongue

the first sip

spilling into a long aaah

that cool first sip of refreshment

© Heather Anne Gordon: 2000 April

blue gums

blue gums rise in soft light

cream flowers spill

against smooth bark

birds come to feed and rest

gumnuts

cupped like wine glasses

holding the spirit of barossa

© Heather Anne Gordon 2016 February

true hearts

in the heart
of the mallee scrub
where wilderness whispers
liney and bec   dreamers
under the callitris

their camp
a sanctuary
beneath an intense night sky

stars burning bright
a haven
amidst the vast expanse

strong women   resilient
as the land they tread

building a life   a community
where hearts
interlace   friends arrive
with caravans and tents

a tapestry of lives   laughter
mingles with the wind

support woven in every thread

by day
they wear many hats
the stress
of work's demands

yet in the mallee's embrace
they find peace
hand in hand   nature's balm

soothes the weary
the wild expanse   so calm

two souls entwined
in the quiet   solace they seek

evenings by the campfire
stories shared

beneath the stars
a sisterhood of wanderers
free spirits

unchained   liney and bec
their bond unbreakable

face the storms   their love a beacon
guiding through
the wilderness unknown

together   they carve out time
sacred moments

to breathe   crafting a life
a refuge   where creativity
finds release   the night sky
intense

a canvas of infinite dreams
just like pleiades
their bodies dance and gleam

in the mallee's wild embrace
they build their paradise

a life of joy and peace
where daily struggles subside

liney and bec
and their friends   community

so strong   in the heart
of the mallee wilderness

they survive and belong

© Heather Anne Gordon: 2025 March

the strain of explaining pain

pain is a whisper

pain is a roar

a fleeting ache

or something far more

a weight unseen

yet heavy to bear

a silent shadow

a breath of despair

© Heather Anne Gordon: 2025 May 10

quiet heart

old trees hold space

hollows

made by time and storm

a soft dark shelter

galahs laugh

kookaburras call

owls dream

possums curl

as well

bats and bees

feed

life waits

and begins again

in the quiet heart

of old trees

© Heather Anne Gordon: 2016 January

shards

fog between vines

cold in my knees

crushed ice joints

salt   wind   mouth

waves   slow   thud

joy and kalika

knife   red   capsicum

seeds   clicking   sink

you hold the key

fence rattling dry wind

tiles snapping like shells

antiseptic clinging   skin

artists' voices

internet connection

dog   fence   wind   stars

a ribbon in the night sky

bonnet club

mornings   iced coffee sweet

bottles   clink   payment

rats in ceiling   silver tin men

glue tacky winter

ebooks wandering smoke

mouse-click   footsteps

walls creek boulders

paper soft cotton

desert rain smell

tin sheds creaking

plastic water containers

lucky foodbank cartons

boots on rock floors

laughter echoing stone

romance scam joke

bread smell spilling

voices flat in ear

urgent voice sharp

thirty thousand house

maps drawn lost

lily retreat

country shifting

sala   ebooks uploaded

seven seasons dust iron

three lilies bloom

appointments   antiseptic

coffee steam curling

new book smell

august sala season

house someone else's dream

basic maths

sixteen births between
eighteen seventy two
and ninety one

thirteen children grown
beneath the seppeltsfield sun

numbers marking a life
where the work was never done

riding the distance

alison rides her bike
with a window view of sky

she calls me and we laugh
about my coach voice
from the couch

our talk rolls hard
through politics and the body

her rage moves the pedals
my rage spills to the page

together we ride the distance
without leaving home

pardalotes

tiny bright pardalotes

flitting among eucalyptus green

they tend the trees

with clever beaks

chip-chip a rising joy

the leaves breathe easier

the land sings with them

eliza arbuckle only eighteen years in
her bones only girlhood behind her
yet the river already asked for more
than girlhood could give hair pinned
against the wind hands soft but not
for long the year eighteen thirty nine
and adelaide's dust still clinging to her
skirts

eliza followed charles and charlotte
sturt up the murray river julia gawler
beside her a child really just fifteen
their laughter and fear swallowed into
the wide silence of river gums
bending like elders listening

they called it exploration they called it
progress but the maps were only
guesses and the boats groaned with
empire's hunger men certain the land
would bow before them yet the river
spoke its own tongue the bush
whispered refusal in the crack of
branches and the shimmer of heat a
living thing pressing its hot mouth
against their breath

henry bryan wandered and was gone
no body no grave only absence left
behind a shadow stitched into soil and
sky his horse stumbling back to
adelaide hooves curled grotesque
with neglect the man himself
scattered into dust or silence never
returned never answered yet a creek
and a mountain named after him

and the women the girls they bent to
smaller tasks water fetched clothes
mended smoke burning their eyes
wounds tended quietly while the men
dreamed of inland seas the women
carried survival in their hands

separated in the heat eliza arbuckle
and isaac hearnshaw and john craig
stumbling back toward adelaide days
measured in thirst and trials until the
sudden fire of accident isaac's
gunpowder flask bursting his face
undone flesh torn his left eye forced
from its place the smell of burning
powder choking the air

but eliza did not falter she held the
ruin of his face her hand steady
against blood and fire she reached for
the dislodged eye and set it back into
its socket no trembling no fainting
only the fierce stillness of someone
remade in that moment not maid not
servant but force calm as river stone
unbroken

and later much later the plaque out
near eudundacowie ngadjuri country
wind rolling over cultivated crops
words carved cold in metal
remembering isaac remembering ruin
and remembering john and
remembering eliza now called friend
not maid not servant but friend as if
the land itself refused the smallness
empire tried to write her into

still the plaque weathers against the
sky layers of history pressing voice
against voice loud ones drowning
others yet eliza breaks through fierce
girl witness steady hand the land
itself whispering her back into
memory

charles sturt chasing his mirage of
inland sea his mount bryan expedition
now a line of words along the
lavender trail three hundred and
twenty five kilometres walked for
leisure by those who come after
walking not for empire but for
pleasure carrying water good maps
laughter instead of inland sea dreams

and eliza later writing herself larger
than life pages swollen with
extravagance carried her story across
oceans to america and beyond then
back again to establish a new school
on the north shore of new south wales
and then in bowden in adelaide with
angas family support shaping her
world with the only book she trusted
a version of the bible and her own fire

eliza arbuckle or davies as she came
to be known after a forced marriage a
girl who pinned her hair against the
wind and walked into hush of river
gums girl who pressed an eye back
into its place who refused to be
erased she breathes still along the
lavender trail along the ngadjuri wind
friend not servant fierce not small her
story a pulse beneath the plaques a
reminder that women too carried
empire's burdens and remade
themselves in the ash and the dust

eliza left no children to speak her
name no descendants to etch their
name with hers so the plaque out
from eudundacowie carries only the
men's descendants with their
bloodlines carrying them forward
while hers is left revealing the
fracture in recorded history where
men are remembered through lineage
and stone while women appear only
in fragments fleeting words scattered
recollections yet their labour their
courage their fierce survival cut deep
only the world mostly forgets them

© Heather Anne Gordon: 2025 September

feral bees

feral bees swarm loud

native wings fade from the bloom

silence in their hive

© Heather Anne Gordon: 2025 October

pain management

she tried to be still

each breath pushing pain

like glass shards

through her body

her bowels

grumbling low warning

too much oxy not enough water

fluids in fluids out

every step to the toilet

was a war

rise from the bed   shuffle

slow   lower onto the seat

strain with the dull ache

of constipation

twist to wipe   rise again

hands soaped in cold water

shuffle back   defeated

earlier

she had swallowed the oxy

with stale water

then shuffled to the shower

imitating the careless stance

of a man's standing piss

the warm water ran over her

but her body

could not stand long

could not bear the weight

of soap

she dragged herself out

pulled on

the only clean nightwear

a garish fleece striped

red and lime

hair wet

electric blanket on high

one dog baleful at the bed's end

the other curled in the heap

of yesterday's clothes

she fell sideways

into a drug haze

rattling at the front door

the dog on the bed

lifting her head

waiting for orders

the screen door shook again

who's there she called

pain rolling through her voice

no answer

again louder *who is it*

then the side gate latch rattled

panic and pain joined hands

the dogs could get out

her dog lost

the visiting dog lost

her friends in vanuatu

how would she explain

she called again

shuffled to the door

body slack with drugs and hurt

opened the wooden door

but clung to its frame

who is it

footsteps pounded closer

a face from years gone

an arm outstretched

with an untidy lump

wrapped in newspaper

slow realisation

of her own untidy lumpiness

and that

she must take it

and if she wanted more

she must call

i can't   i i i can't

her tongue refused the rest

the visitor glared

turned away   stormed off

next time ring before you come
she managed

triumph bloomed for a moment

but her hands betrayed her

the door slammed hard

its echo a sharp insult in the air

she turned

towards the bedroom

saw her reflection in the mirror

a huge body

in red and lime stripes

speckled with yellow cactus

a pink crease

across her pale face

hair flat on one side

vertical on the other

laughter tore from her belly

pain bursting

with each convulsion

sobs tangled with giggles

until she collapsed on the bed

in a heap of ridiculous agony

© Heather Anne Gordon: 2010 July

ikanga mulka

a lovely day beneath the sky
at bethany
where water tumbles

ikanga mulka
words we hold
we sit   we talk
as stories unfold

we share through food
through art   through stories

through every voice
where hearts are strong

the sun as witness all day long
our lives entwined
in preliminaries

with smoke
that rose in gentle sway
ngadjuri led the way today

an acknowledgement
firm and true
to those who walked
this land we knew

ngadjuri kaurna peramangk kin
their wisdom carried
deep within
their ancient stories
shared again

the children came
with hearts open wide
and grown-ups knelt
right by their side

clay took shape
and seeds were strung
on threads of meaning
old yet young

paint met canvas
and symbols grew
as art gave voice
to something true
a culture shared in every hue

barossa bushgardens
brought to light
the leaves that soothe
the medicine with might

each one a story
green and bold
medicinal culinary ancient told
a gift from soil
both wise and old

the plates were full
the hearts were fed
with native spice
and ancient bread

the hospitality crew
with thoughtful care
brought flavours anew
strong and rare
vegan   meat and gluten-free
a menu shaped by history
food as bridge for you and me

beyond the voices soft and clear
a quiet space drew people near
with printed word
and screen aglow
to let the deeper learning flow
reflection found a silent room
where thoughts could bud
and knowledge bloom
a quiet space
where truth made room

the tables dressed in fibre wood
a blend
of old and new that stood
we may not know
each artist's name
but through their touch
the friendship came

traditional lines in modern grace
each leaf each flower
held time and place
a shared design
for shared space

© Heather Anne Gordon 2024 April 21

mallee

there is plenty of energy
stored in the lignotubers

mallee areas
are generally very flat

without hills   or tall trees

it is very easy to become lost

there is a lot of bare ground

and any leaf litter decomposes

slowly   in the dry conditions

long thin strips of bark drop off

and resemble wriggle sticks

mallee is a complex

and sensitive environment

as am i

sitting amongst the mallee

in a comfortable chair

with my mates

i do not see them often enough

we catch up on family news

sad news of friends

upcoming dates

they talk of future adventures

my mates

are planning on camping

and driving interstate

my stored energy

comes surging to the surface

as i strive to tell my stories

about a road trip adventure

forty years ago   camping

with two kids

aged twelve and nine

and two dogs and paper maps

no mobile phones   no g p s

but my adventures

are in the past

theirs are in the future

they are hopeful   i am dismal

unlike the mallee

i have no stores of energy left

© Heather Anne Gordon 2024 April 5

we begin by remembering

before eighteen thirty-six

the first peoples lived here

their footsteps their fire

their song in the wind

this land never empty

never nobody's

always held always sung

always known

in eighteen thirty-four

letters patent

spoke of truth on paper

acknowledging ancient care

and belonging

yet settlers turned away

colonists ignored the promise

blood spilled without protest

across river and plain

massacres mapped on the soil

pain stitched deep into memory

in eighteen ninety-four

the women stood strong

in eighteen ninety-six

ngarrindjeri women

claimed the right

to write their names

to mark their choice

the women insisted on voting

the first in this country

the fourth in the world

their voices refusing erasure

laws shifted slowly

nineteen sixty-six

aboriginal lands trust

nineteen eighty-one

pitjantjatjara land rights

nineteen eighty-four

maralinga tjarutja land rights

each step a fragment of justice

still unfinished still burning

mabo spoke

in nineteen ninety-two

native title breaking the lie

terra nullius undone

truth rising

like smoke from country

in twenty twenty-three

australia was asked to listen

to recognise to give voice

yet the referendum

revealed our failure

the no vote spoke louder

than compassion

a country turning away

once more

denying truth denying justice

a wound reopened

across the continent

proof that unfinished business

remains

that reconciliation

without action

is hollow

to acknowledge country

is to remember all of this

to feel the weight

of ancient hands on stone

to honour survival

custodianship   knowledge

tools   fire   weaving

medicine   stars

trade and story lines

crossing the land

the oldest continuous culture

on this earth

to acknowledge

is to accept the gift

to know that this nation

is layered

ancient and recent

braided together

to face unfinished business

to seek justice still denied

to walk

listening

learning

leaning

toward the truth

that was always here

© Heather Anne Gordon: 2023 October

sarah

generous one we asked for recipes
how to cook pigeon on the bbq
introduced me to quiche she laughed
that chortling laugh earth mother
feminist kind and clever gardener and
keeper of chooks referrer of good
books loving patient mother her
warmth still hums whenever i hear
the travelling wilburys we had it on
repeat during our long trip to the
coorong her care still grows in us all
sunlight resting gentle
08/10/1951 – 09/12/2021

© Heather Anne Gordon: 2021 December

hospital

my friend
lies in the white hum
of the hospital

waiting for a machine
that sounds like
a deep sea place

bariatric chamber
they call it

a room for divers
when their blood
has forgotten
how to breathe

neither of us
know exactly what
it will feel like

so i tell her
she can drift away in her mind
slip below the surface
and find the mermaids

are there brown mermaids
she asks
yes i say *i am sure there are*
and i go looking
in the museum archives
i find them

yawkyawk they are called
in the country
of western arnhem land

women from the waist up
fish from the waist down
scales glinting in billabongs
and streams

they keep the water clean
for drinking
call the rains with their voices
sometimes the rain is kind
sometimes it comes as flood
and hunger
so they are loved and feared
in the same breath

i tell kitty
she can imagine the yawkyawk
floating in the cool shade
of pandanus palms

their hair drifting
like dark weed in slow water
their eyes holding
the whole history of this land

if she is quiet
they might let her pass
or even cradle her in the water
until the fear floats out of her

she can let the hum
of the machine
be the hum of the current

let the walls of the chamber
be the skin of a deep pool

until the breath
comes easy again

needs vs luxuries

the cost of living
a pressing weight

as ticket prices soar
at an opulent gate

to impress or nourish
a choice we state

abstain for excellence
or spend to create

in this dance of life
we contemplate

in high-priced chaos
we might strain
music festival splurges
status reigns
seek sustenance
or flaunt the gain

or abstain

excellence to attain
in life's mad dance

do values wane

balancing needs
and dreams to chase
essentials first
or luxury's embrace

basic needs or splurges
we survey
a balance sought
come what may

in choices made
our values on display
in envy's shade
we tread so light
basic needs
our daily fight
with gratitude our hearts
take flight

we seek
contentment's gentle sight
balancing dreams
with life's unjust might

in summer's blaze
the world is harsh
only a car for shelter
nights so sparse

poverty's grip
a daily march
resilience demands
a burning arch
hope's ember shines
even within the parched

cost of living
strains the heart
essentials   luxuries
we drift apart
choices weigh
each plays a part

poverty's grip   resilience's art
in life's balance
challenges start
they tear us apart

© Heather Anne Gordon: 2025 January 22

huntsman spiders

huntsman
move silent under bark
long legs
stretch across
the shadowed wall

they do not claim fear
though we tremble
they are patient keepers
of balance

feeding on the night's
crawling hunger
like cockroaches and crickets

in the barossa
they drift across dashboards

a sudden shape
against glass
and steering wheel

yet with a cup and paper
gentle hands guide them
to outside rooms of air and tree
reminding us
that even what startles
can still be a neighbour
in the dark

© Heather Anne Gordon: 2016 May

wongaburra

i was led astray

yesterday

wongaburra called me

once cropping land

now corrugated soil

stone chips and weeds mown

but before it was cleared

for grain crops

it was bushland

again there are native plants

in the ground

some home grown

no trees to cast shade

but we wanted to chat

we sat in the caravan's shadow

around the back

three pastry slices

from truro's bakery

sweet

apple   apricot   custard

oh   what a treat

iced coffee cooled my core

while surely

the hot coffee heated

shaz and andrea more

shifting to the four-wheel

drive's shade

warm winds stirred

willy willy

whirlwinds played

my phone

left in the car's warm embrace

four hours later

a temperature warning

on its face

me

sunburned

windburned

dehydrated

alas

but the conversations out there

a splendid contrast

despite knowing better

the chat did not slack

today was a rest day

to get my energy back

thinking about

eucalypt plantings

on the right track

if there is a next time

u v protection   i will pack

stubble quail

stubble quail
hiding quiet in the grass

soft brown flecks
against the earth

sudden thunder of wings
breaks the stillness

startled hearts rise with them
into sky

tassie hangover

i got home late
ache-late brain-lagged
blunt-edged tired

the kind of tired
where your body
might be a loose agreement
your limbs made
without consulting you

five a m start
late-night finish
that kind of maths
does not end well

consequently
i dropped a container of milk
on the floor
not threw   not spilled
dropped
like it just slipped
from my timeline

cloud cleaned that up
enthusiastically
like it was a service
she was born to provide

i still have to mop today
when my spine
feels like it is strung together
with coat hangers
and stinging nettles

but later

currants

whole damn packet
on the same floor
just as sticky

you cannot trust dogs
with dried fruit
currants
toxic little time bombs

can cause depression and death

    how poetic
same could be said of me
after two glasses of red

so i swept them
barefoot   defeated
sticky soles
sweeping like a ghost
of domestic failure

trying not to cry
about raisins
on a cold vinyl floor

and outside
fog
days of it
grey
pressed against the window
like a sad face

all my clothes are on the line
have been since tassie
nothing is dry
everything is limp
and i loathe   loathe
double-handling clothes

do not make me touch
those damp jeans again
do not

so the real question is
do i go clothes shopping
is this how it starts
tired   fogged-out
fermented   fruitless

i wander into a shop and buy
synthetic socks
and a slightly-too-shiny
fleece jacket
because it is dry
and my clothes are not

this is my tassie hangover
not the wine   not the travel
but the world i came back to
damp   chaotic
carpeted in currants
and consequence

this is the poetry
of being too tired
to fold your life back into shape

kangaroo grass

kangaroo grass
holds on roadside edges

tussocky   stubborn
through heat and dust

rusty blades
shimmer in the summer glare

ngadjuri soil
remembers its strength

brown mermaids

brown mermaids
live in the shadows
of waterholes

they shimmer
in the heat haze
of the dry season

tails flashing
like rusted bronze
under a sun that burns the skin

eyes deep with knowing
older than the sky

they move
with the grace of rain
on cracked earth

whispers curling
like smoke
through paperbark trees

you can hear them
if you listen   in the breathless
hour before dawn

when the wind
holds its tongue
and the frogs hush

they are keepers
of the billabong
the vein of life in thirsty land

they bless the thirsty
and curse the careless

their hands
can cup the cool drink
you have searched for days
or close the water's face
over your head forever

brown mermaids
are not the fairy tale ones
of foreign seas
no seashell crowns
no laughing foam

they wear shadows
for skirts
and river mud
for armour

their hair floats
like eel grass
curling in dark currents

they live
between blessing
and vengeance

between the first drop of rain
and the flood that takes the hut

between the memory
of old songs
and the silence
of drowned country

their beauty a trap
their love a warning

and still
we ache to see them
to know their voices
and survive the telling

for in the deep of our longing
we believe we might be spared

© Heather Anne Gordon: 2021 December

my frog bog

out in the dark with my phone and
torch the night alive with hidden
voices banjo frogs thrum alive in the
frog bog plonk plonk like laughter
under water their calls rise and ripple
through the cold air i record each
sound for the frog id project sending
songs to the australian museum small
acts of science stitched with wonder
proof that care can sound like music
in the night

© Heather Anne Gordon: 2017 November

194

catalyst

i am not receptive
to your talk of nociceptors
i do not want to learn
about pain

i just want it gone

i know that story
about how opioids affect

my thinking

my quality of life

my risk of falls

an *accidental* overdose

the fear-avoidance model
seems common sense
it hurts to move = do not move
the downward spiral
consequence
learning about pain   i resist
involved   i might persist

it is my physio   the optimist

the catalyst

insists

assists

recites the lorimer playlist

i might as well
go along with this

© *Heather Anne Gordon: 2025 May 15*

grasses

native grasses

bend with wind and time

grazed by kangaroos

their seed taken by finches

caterpillars feed

and butterflies rise

quail and other small birds

swell the ground with life

© Heather Anne Gordon: 2016 October

allocasuarina verticillata

drooping sheoak
its needles whisper weather
fine music for wind to play
beneath it
the soil remembers
and the shadows speak in olive grey

© Heather Anne Gordon: 2017 September

lindley lies quiet within the mid
murray council a stretch north of
morgan where the goyder highway
only brushes the edge its bitumen line
grazing the south western corner as
though hurrying past

its boundaries were drawn not so
long ago with lines on a map to match
the hundred of lindley county of burra
named in eighteen eighty-one for john
lindley botanist dreamer librarian to
sir joseph banks professor in london
who never walked this dust yet whose
name carried across oceans to take
root here

settlers came in that same year
eighteen eighty-one when survey
lines cut the country open when
closer settlement was declared they
bought land for a pound an acre the
government gazette inked their
names neat as if promise could be
listed so plainly credit was offered
time was granted they were told
improve this soil and make it pay
before the debt comes due

yet the land remembered other
caretakers and the winds across this
country told stories older than any
survey peg older than any acre price
and the earth held both silence and
resistance as fences rose and
homesteads faltered

yesterday i went there with deb she
drove and i opened the gates to the
cemetery paddock for us to creep
inside and there we saw the cairn of
limestones stacked in a corner quiet
testament that a church once stood
there twenty fourth april eighteen
eighty six a school too opened eighth
august eighteen eighty seven and held
on until the last day of december
nineteen twenty two the blue painted
sign announcing all this as if I could
possibly do the maths

lindley now a locality with a name
heavy with history of botany of banks
of bargains struck and sometimes
broken still lies north of morgan its
paddocks stitched with memory its
air carrying echoes of both settlement
and loss

in lindley the wind keeps secrets in
the dry grass the stones remember
footsteps the night breathes with the
voices of those who once walked and
once loved there is a ghost who
moves slowly between the old church
ruins and the rigid grid of the
graveyard some say she was a woman
who came from the east from lands
where rivers were green and full of
eels some say she fled hunger some
say she fled a man others whisper she
was the hunger herself she was the
fire in her own body she was the one
who walked at night to gather herbs
when the village slept who whispered
to the wedge tail eagles who let the
lambs live when the farmers called for
slaughter she was the one who would
not bow

the people in lindley feared her

because she did not stay inside the

fences she did not keep her words soft

she did not choose a husband when

one was chosen for her she did not

kneel to the pastor she was seen

walking beneath the moon hair

undone feet bare carrying small

bundles of roots and bones she lit

fires in the scrub and sang low the

kind of singing that makes the skin

prickle the kind of singing that makes

men restless in their sleep

one day she was gone some say she

drowned in the creek swollen after

storm some say she walked into the

west and never came back some say

the men came for her with rope and

hate and a need to silence the wild but

no one speaks that aloud in daylight

only in hushed tones at dusk

the ghost of lindley lingers still she
walks in the shimmer of heat over the
barren paddocks she slips through the
dust that follows the sheep she curls
herself into the smoke of rollies she is
seen sometimes in the corner of the
eye a woman shape shadow thick with
silence she does not weep she does not
scream she only waits she only
watches those who stayed in lindley
long enough knew her presence they
said the dogs howled when she passed
they said milk turned sour in the billy
tea they said the wind rattled the iron
roof harder when she was near but
some said if you walk to her gently if
you meet her at the cemetery gate
when the moon is silver she will press
something into your hand a stone a
feather a bone and if you keep it safe if
you do not betray her gift you will find
the strength to stand outside fences
you will find the courage to refuse you
will learn to walk your own ground

in lindley the ghost is not gone she is

not defeated she is the breath that

softly carries the word aaaah into the

night she is the lesson that no matter

what is done to silence one woman

the earth remembers and the earth

keeps her voice

after womad

i kept my promise
to myself
no womad this year
the drums the dance
the dust of botanic park
held in memory
not in motion

but joy came anyway
idgie at her side
tail wagging
at the promised reunion
friday joy dropped idgie off
thursday night
joy came back   sun-browned
and festival-fed

ready to paddle
at blanchetown
where river breathes
in limestone cliffs
where pelicans
once filled the air
like feathered thunder
but now only whispers remain
tom charted a course
and we followed
like slow-moving fire
in the afternoon sun
this is no lazy drift
this is pull   and reach
sinew-strain
through the murray water's
resistance
paddles bite
muscles answer
wind slaps
we do not flinch
joy steady at kalika's side
voice calm   hands sure
kalika listens leans learns
and smiles
that wide grin of the newly-bold
first time in a kayak
first time feeling
what it means
to steer your own direction
on the water

i stayed behind for a time
camera in hand
watching joy kalika and tom
carve silence   into wake
idgie
wriggling with excitement
tail like a flag
feet scrabbling at water's edge
trying to herd the entire river
into order
later   cloudie and i
paddled across to the cliffs
those cathedral bones
of time and tide
few pelicans this time
tom says
they have flown to kati thanda
answering the call
of floodwater dreams
from queensland skies
but black swans still sang
in silhouettes
and ducks carved ribbons
in the quiet
by day's end
we were river-heavy
sun-slowed
salted with tired smiles

we left tom
to cook by his own fire
while the rest of us
drove back
toward nuriootpa night
vintner's bar and grill
nearly nine   hungry
sun worn   not looking flash
but welcomed
like wanderers returning
from an odyssey
we sat like conquerors
not of land   but of effort
of kilometres paddled
of storms resisted
of promises kept
joy shouted dinner
payment she said
for idgie's keep
but really
it was a shared feast
for old friendship
new adventure
and the deep breath
of water-earned hunger

© Heather Anne Gordon: 2007 March 16

banksias

banksias
stand like corner stores of gold

feeding honey eaters
precious nectar bold

possums climb
where blossoms
pour sweet light

insects hum deep into the night

bronzewing pigeons
nest safe in their hold

© Heather Anne Gordon: 2016 March

blue banded bees

blue banded bees shimmer

in the barossa sun

their stripes a song of teal and black

they hover hum dart among blossoms

each flower kissed awake

by their gentle weight

© Heather Anne Gordon: 2016 April

days blur
under endless forms
and demands
in a system
that fragments life
into charts and commands

stiff bureaucracy
stifles more
than physical pain
assuming we exist
solely
in our constrained domain

burdened
by red tape that steals time
meant for care
ignoring our work
our families
the full passions we bear

living under assumptions
our potential talent erased
in distant offices or home
our truths remain misplaced

time spent on administration
dims the light inside
yet   resilient and defiant
our vibrant lives will not hide

© Heather Anne Gordon: 2025 June 1

cloud

hillacre hawaiian cloud
blue merle
with eyes like clear sky
after rain
calm as morning tide
born to the show ring
proud and obedient in her stride
but choosing her own finish
eventually

once around the ring
was enough for her
no need to circle twice
for the sake of applause

then the breeding years
when she came into my life
she flew to sydney
for a wild copulation
arrangement

and i told my sydney son
such things
had never happened to me
he laughed and said
don't stay with me then

and after one last litter
cloud was mine in name
and in heart

we took long road trips
in the car   with a window seat
not in a trailer with other dogs

she learned the shimmer
of kayak water
the gentle weight of a hand
with pet partner therapy
the art of making friends
wherever she stood
cloud was a beacon
in any crowd

she once walked alone
through the dark
graetztown to stockwell
while i was away
a journey that left us all raw
with relief and love

she welcomed idgie
with open joy
welcomed everyone
with the same
my brother tom called her
my favourite niece

and they kayaked together
along the murray at big bend
the photos still warm my heart

she was perfect for me
except for the way her fur
collected every prickle
on fossil hunting days
a small price for such beauty

cloud had many adventures
and when her time came
the sky felt wider
but quieter too

© Heather Anne Gordon: 2020 August

journalling

in the quiet rebellion
of every word written
i reclaim my script   each scar
each silent chapter
rewritten into verses
of occasional optimism
this illness   just a stanza
in the epic of who i am
yields to a narrative of power
i redefine my truth
one bold   liberated
line at a time
despite its attempts to erase
a third of my lifetime

© Heather Anne Gordon: 2025 April 25

port moorowie

april 2017

narungga country

beach wind salt on my skin

mparntwe friends

joy and kalika

their voices

layered over the hum of sea

i had driven

from the barossa valley

ngadjuri peramangk kaurna

country

cold settling into my bones

psoriatic arthritis

gnawing from the inside

frost and fog

lying low along the bare vines

i said i could not face

another barossa winter

kalika

looking up

from the chopping board

said

you hold the key to that

heather

and a window opened

broken hill in new south wales

glittered like an idea

i drove back

to the folds of the valley

thinking of a sky

wider than my pain

barossa valley

april 2017

emails to my sons

subject line

you might be surprised

or even shocked

sydney said *no*

seattle said *no*

sydney spoke of my doctors

my nurses

the allied health web

keeping me alive

seattle said

buy warmer clothes

get a sad light

spend money on electricity

instead

buy a van travel in winter

sydney offered

too many reasons not to

too many weights

holding me still

and then andamooka

drifted into the conversation

thirty thousand for a house

sydney son set the deal

three winters and we reassess

i was already seeing red dunes

in my dreams

andamooka

july and august 2017

sala workshops

new faces new hands

shaping colour

under wide blue skies

sunrises molten pink

milky way heavy with light

like it could tumble

into my open hands

searching for a house

falling in love

with the impractical

stone walls

boulders from a creek bed

ventilation shafts

tin men

waving arms in the wind

deceased estate full of ghosts

rats and dust and stories

i said *yes*

my body said *maybe*

my heart said *now*

barossa valley

april 2018

electrician's invoice

another reminder

that dreams

come with wires and codes

and levies

reality bites

but i keep moving

andamooka

april to october 2018

friends

helping hands on every job

levelling dirt

for my unsteady steps

handrails bolted by ben

bonnet club mornings

iced coffee gossip

and who can fix the shit pit

afternoons chasing views

in chado's ute

evenings learning

to bend metal into form

teaching mosaic in the sunporch

art on the fence

reclaimed wire fibre steel glass

remote area nurses

steadying my health

art steadying my mind

barossa valley

november 2018 to march 2019

planning mosaics for sala

for andamooka

another surgery

at last the special boot

is gone from my foot

andamooka

april to october 2019

head full of colour and dust

governor visit

community celebration

knocking on doors

mapping the artists

diverse hands diverse stories

art unfurled in a hall

a hall carried from maralinga

bonnet club

not just chatter

but quiet saving of lives

coober pedy

september 2019

meeting with old friends

old ground

plans made

under the dog fence sky

valued in a shared purpose

voices stretching

toward the world

andamooka

october 2019

chado asked

what sydney son would think

of the spending

i sent the romance scam text

i could be in a foreign prison
labelled a drug mule
mixed up in a romance scam

in an instant came

the romance scam reply

that whole house
is a romance scam

chado and i laughed

then medical tides

dragged me back to the barossa

barossa valley

November 2019 to march 2020

writing bonnet club book

corona virus moving closer

rheumatologist said *stay home*

lockdown sealed the valley

skype with grandson hours long

friends leaving fresh vegetables

at my door

sourdough made

papers shredded

collages born

from old photographs

concertina books for children

bonnet club story moved online

adult novel *desert deluge*

carrying andamooka

in my veins

when i could not touch its dust

andamooka

july to october 2021

arriving into lockdown

maps

showing where i could walk

though my joints kept me still

water delivery

foodbank cartons

humbling in their weight

sala planning

pushing through rules

record number of entries

metal fence and walls

alive with art

hashtags pasted vertical

turning rage into a collage book

three eye surgeries

desert deluge edited

with friends' eyes and hands

barossa valley

january to december 2022

doctors shaking heads

covid risk

keeping me away

from the outback

nineteen artists four exhibitions

in a town

of two hundred and sixty-two

creatives resilient as mulga

satisfying

to see the art fence fill

year after year

barossa valley

may to july 2023

helping artists

shape their words

their prices

their confidence

collage canvases

went north without me

mentoring liz with

her grandfather's journals

adelaide

december 2023

sydney son

said it was time

to let the house go

i know

it had already given me

andamooka

the people   the arid light

the art   the freedom

barossa valley

august 2024

ebooks continuing

erratic as my breath

last andamooka sala

turkey gratitude books

easy to carry

seven seasons of sala

in andamooka

a title in itself

stories recorded

of trish

mary

liz   and liv

bonnet club online

both andamooka lily

and outback lily

verses born from the red dirt

now an artist   author

children's book creator

with a page on the web

barossa valley

august 2025

seven seasons gone

the andamooka house

now someone else's

romance project

fulltime in the valley

medical appointments

writing   collage

online chats with friends

online sala

but just one physical artwork

at nuriootpa library

amongst the shelves

attending workshops

led by others

a follower now

Heather Anne Gordon 2025 August

psoriatic arthritis

it started with a whisper

a subtle little itch

then came the swelling

life's sneaky little glitch

a sly disease

with a cunning disguise

it tiptoes in quietly

then pounces   surprise

it will not play fair

it changes the rules

it ridicules

and enables the ghouls

lily plots and plans

adjusts and persists

yet psoriatic arthritis insists

lily   you cannot resist!

oh   it comes with a posse

a co-morbidity gang

fatigue   depression

and joints that harangue

diabetes tries to edge in

with the liver not pleased

osteoporosis sneaks up

the lungs start to wheeze

but lily has tactics

she knows the game

can she outfox the disease

or will she drown in self- blame

her body ravaged

by relentless pain

defiance crumbles

fragile honesty

that shattering stillness

humbles

clematis microphylla

old man's beard drifts
soft against the wind

seed clusters
feathered white wings

tender offerings
to birds building homes

beneath the bushy green
shelter of its arms

leaves warmed
and pressed to skin

healing held
in the quiet touch of earth

© Heather Anne Gordon: 2016 November

bush stone curlew

stone curlew calling
long curdling cry
moonlit scrub
ghost of the long plains

© Heather Anne Gordon: 2000 September

andamooka

out on the edge
of the ancient eromanga sea

where time's brushstrokes
linger in sun-drenched hues

the soil cradles secrets
fossils of forgotten epochs

opalised whispers
of creatures long vanished

beneath the arid sun
machines jerk the earth

seeking relics
of a primordial romance

the waltz of ammonites

trilobites

and ancient plants

their stories illustrated
in iridescent opal fire

and there

amidst the hallucinatory heat
amazing mermaids
weave their silent spells

their scales glitter

their eyes glow
from unfathomable depths
custodians of forgotten songs
and underground seas

they rise from the ochre dust
half-dream
half-memory

their gleeful laughter
echoing through eons
for they remember

when the eromanga sea
bathed their scales
and stars whispered
secrets
into their moon-kissed hair

but beware
curious miner
for mermaids are fickle
they lure you with promises
their voices like wind chimes

as the chink of metal sounds
against the level
and when you dig further
they pull you in
to a lusty embrace

when you dig
deep into the sun-baked soil
and unearth the echoes
of eras past
perhaps
just perhaps
you will glimpse them
the mermaids
agents of opalised dreams

as the sun sets
over the eromanga sea's edge
their scales flicker
like constellations
their eyes hold the weight
of forgotten times
and they draw you in to sing
a haunting melody
of longing and obsession

for on the edge of memory
where fossils meet myth
the mermaids swim
eternal and elusive
their opal hearts
pulsing with the rhythm of ages
and the great artesian basin
whispers

please look after me

© Heather Anne Gordon: 2023 April 22

andamooka anna
tilts her head sharp as a crow
quick eyes quick tongue
the kind to cut and stitch
in the same moment

her sisters
andamooka nanna
and barossa nanna
lean in beside her

none of them real enough
for print
but real enough for the children
who wait for the next ebook

about magpie swoopings
and dogs
about chooks and collage
and garden bugs

their kin bloom
under other names

outback lily

andamooka lily

barossa lily

each rooted in the soil of
different times
but bound by the same wind

outback lily steps first
she has no patience
for polite verse or tidy lines

she comes from an old folder marked
for my blog when i get time
she walks like she knows
the page belongs to her
she carries rage
not like a weight but like a torch
its flame steady
through surgeries
through the replacement
of psoriatic arthritis joints
through the slow beat
of a stubborn heart
through the crackles in lungs
with pleural plaques
through the shadows
that lean in when days run long

andamooka lily
blooms wide in red dust

barossa lily
bends with the green vines
of the valley

their words spill into journals
meant for grown ups
grown ups who have not
forgotten

how to listen to wind
how to feel the story
in the grit between their teeth

the rage is still here
older than the newest pain
you can hear it
in the way the pen moves
in the way a line refuses
to bow to convention

but it is not rage
that burns everything
it is rage that keeps walking
shuffle step by shuffle step
with the health team
like a quiet beat
in the background

because there is no romance
in pretending
only in telling it true

and so they write
stubborn lily sisters
sisters in the dust
and the vine
still blooming
still telling
because the stories
are still theirs to hold

feijoa

feijoa fruit

some love

some disdain

a drought-hardy shrub

brought

to australia's terrain

red and green flowers

bring christmas cheer

feijoas are ready

a late autumn treat is here

possibly possums

thursday

no rain   lips of clouds
pressed tight

but wind danced
loud   bold in flight

not a drop spilled
from nature's tilted bowl

yet every leaf twitched
to the wind's harsh toll

friday

twelve-point-six millimetres
the rain arrived

with cold   so sharp
i barely survived

the wind did not whisper
it shrieked and swore

like truths exposed
from a hidden drawer
in the kitchen

saturday

rain came harder
twenty-three-point-eight

each drop a drumbeat
to seal drought's fate

wicking beds brimmed
with the sky's liquid gift

the wind remained relentless
refused to lift

sunday

just spitty rain between
a sunbeam's tease

a fleeting warm light
in the storm's unease

i stepped outside
feet kissed sludge

wicking beds swollen
with sky-fed flood
life giving sky juice

wicking beds once blocked
now freed

water flows slowly
for plant roots in need

the white wicking bed
sat quiet and pale

tomato plants survived
autumn frost and hail
no gardener's hand
sowed them there

just nature whispering
grow if you dare

my backyard
clues viewed
from the kitchen sink
yesterday i gazed over
the sink's thin screen

saw bulbous shapes
of soft tangerine
thought fungi grew
in shadow's hue

but it was mandarin peel
freshly chewed

morning test
more appeared today
like citrus ghosts
bright orange curls of skin
signposts
the ground told stories
of scattered zest
a citrusy crime scene
for me to test

midnight marauders
half-eaten lemons
clues galore
each bite a secret
of backyard lore
my detective mind
pieced the plot
no human hand
no clever bot

the detective detecting

i might have possums
imagine the thrill
citrus bandits in the nightly chill

do they crunch on lemons raw?

or suck mandarin innards in awe?

could they be my tree-top guests

wearing velvet masks and cozy vests?

earthquake detection

while i chased peel
and wicking bed flows
the earth shivered   softly
down below

at ten thirty-eight a subtle quake
but i missed it   despite
being wide awake

too deep in citrus-logic schemes
where garden plots
unfold in themes

decision = possums

so call it a weather report
from the backyard beat

where raindrops rhyme
and possums eat

each spitty sprinkle   each gusty
windy   shout

gives life to tales we rarely talk about

it is just my backyard   but listen
blossoms

it hums with mystery
complete with possums

© Heather Anne Gordon: 2025 July 27

tiliqua rugosa

sleepy lizard
broad tongue blue as summer sky
slow mover
sun-soaked philosopher
guarding the gravel tracks
like an old friend in no hurry

© Heather Anne Gordon: 2005 November

concertina

i woke early   pain

at oh-it-hurts

four thirty

thought

about things

for a bit

decided

to

get on with it

a concertina

collage

book

about a dog

and a

lost ball

how quirky

Heather Anne Gordon: 2025 January 19

one day

every year

the same damn thing

international women's day

the school assembles

the hashtags trend

real men are feminists

women are people too

wow   groundbreaking

captains in blazers

give speeches with borrowed fire

projecting shocking stats
like they mean it

while boys scroll under the desk

or smirk
like the punchline is coming soon

and it always does

because tomorrow

march ninth   we vanish again

you wear a purple ribbon

but call me a slut in the corridor

you show up to the cupcake stall

but tell your mates i am a tease

when i will not smile on command

you talk about empowerment

but whistle at me at the bus stop

tell me again

how you support equality

it is not enough

it was never enough

one day of pretend

does not erase
three hundred and sixty-four

of silence

of locker room jokes

of messages i never asked for

of *whore* yelled across the oval

because i blocked your goal

when i was eleven

my best friend was slut-shamed

for breathing wrong

at twelve

we were too much and not enough

at the same time

sluts for dating

prudes for not

lesbians

if we dared to ignore you

thirteen

first unsolicited nude

i felt the shame

though i did nothing wrong

fourteen

deleted my socials

too much inbox filth

wrapped in the lie of

take it as a compliment

spoiler alert   it never was

fifteen

changed my route to school

to avoid a pack of boys

who barked like dogs

when i dared to walk alone

now i am sixteen

and i have watched
those same mouths

bite into i w d cupcakes

and speak

like they invented respect

i am tired

tired of speeches

of slogans

of branded posts

that burn bright on one day

and ghost us the next

tired of boys being praised

for doing the bare minimum

while we do
the emotional heavy lifting

every single day

the worst part

they believe they are doing enough

society told them so

taught them that feminism is

a performance

not a practice

an aesthetic

not a commitment

and those boys will grow into men

who flinch at the word feminism

who mock it

who weaponize it

who forget that we are

still fighting

but i have not given up

because this

this is fixable

you want to help

then do the work

talk when no one is watching

call out your mates

listen

change

not once

not on march eighth

every   damn   day

so no

you do not get a cupcake

for showing up once a year

you do not get praise

for whispering *equality*

when it is convenient

show me

in your actions

in your choices

in your silence

when you should speak

and in your voice when it counts

we are not your afterthought

we are not your learning curve

we are not your one-day cause

we are here

we are loud

we are tired

and we are done

waiting

© Heather Anne Gordon: 2008 March

january twenty-six

a date that makes hearts ache

not all find joy

for some

it is hard to take

in australia

a reminder of wounds and inequality

for first nations peoples

these celebrations cut deep

acknowledge history

celebrate diversity

respect and understanding
make us free

Heather Anne Gordon: 2025 January 26

mistletoe

mistletoe clings with sticky seed

gift of the bird who eats then feeds

a parasite yes but also grace

life carried forward branch to place

a story of hunger and need

in late summer when flowers are few

mistletoe blossoms

for birds to pursue

nectar sweet in the hottest light

dense green shade a nesting site

a refuge where survival grew

on roadside gums the clusters spread

too many mouths where few are fed

scarcity makes the balance bend

yet even in burden the trees still lend

their arms for life to thread

© Heather Anne Gordon: 2016 December

probably rats

death aisle mitre ten with tina
ta-da ta-ta-da ta-ta-da ta-ta-da
possum dream rat truth
ta-da ta-ta-da ta-ta-da ta-ta-da
bright box small shroud
la-la-la-la   la-la-la-la
hollow citrus hollow heart
la-la-la-la   la-la-la-la

standing with tina in the death aisle
i feel my feet slump into tiled grief
and into my brain
comes a crooked refrain
running wild in the pharmacy aisle
from blossom nineteen ninety-four
and i wonder what it means
to hum this
ta-da ta-ta-da ta-ta-da ta-ta-da
while my fingers hover
over neat blue boxes of death

tell me a lie

the less i know the better i feel

slides in like a silk scarf

through my ribs

choosing the mode of death

for rats feels heavy

like i am feeding a shadow in my chest

will owls sweep the night sky

to carry away the dying

i doubt it

or there would be no rats at all

on facebook i bragged

possums had come to me

gutted lemons bright skins

left to rot in the grass

but doubt moved in like cold wind

under the door

sam told me about the scats

about the truth i did not want

rats he said *plain as the weather*

and doreen said *trust sam*

still i wanted possums

more than anything

possum teeth choose rind over flesh

rat teeth leave hollowed ghosts

of citrus

this is the difference

between mercy and hunger

and now i am holding the bright box

thinking of sunday back in ninety-four

la-la-la-la   la-la-la-la

and tina beside me

silent like the aisle itself

as i choose a small shroud

for creatures i cannot love

ta-da ta-ta-da ta-ta-da ta-ta-da

ta-da ta-ta-da ta-ta-da ta-ta-da

la-la-la-la   la-la-la-la

la-la-la-la   la-la-la-la

© Heather Anne Gordon: 2025 August 4

mermaids

in the depths where coral blooms

where moonlight kisses azure waves

dwells a sisterhood of mermaids

silent warriors of salt and foam

they smile   not in surrender

but defiance   pearl-lipped rebellion

as misogyny swirls like tempests

churning tides of ancient bias

their tails shimmer with resilience

scales forged from whispered courage

for they know the currents well

challenges surge

but so does strength

each cresting wave   a battle won

each ebb   a chance to redefine

they weave their stories into kelp

an anthem for the silenced voices

and when the sun dips low

painting the horizon in fiery hues

these mermaids rise   unyielding

making changes in their watery realm

their sea   a canvas

of transformation

where patriarchal storms dissipate

and the tides echo their defiance

we are more than myths

we are change

so   let the waves bear witness

as mermaids swim through adversity

smiling   resolute   unbroken

in their small section of the sea

© Heather Anne Gordon: 2024 May

echidna

spike-back wanderer
nose down to the earth's heart
each step a soft excavation
of old knowing   of patient love

© Heather Anne Gordon: 2005 October

hardenbergia violacea

the happy wanderer

once climbed the fence

violet and green trails

of barossa bushgarden sense

former neighbour and i

planting with care

a promise of green life

we would share

birds and insects

drifting through

native sarsaparilla

but the new neighbour came

with hose in hand

dreams of a cottage garden

shaped his land

digging where roots had tried to stay

he mounded earth

in an old-fashioned way

fertiliser heavy poured against my say

now the fence lies bare

where violet colour once ran

soil turned heavy beneath his hand

blood and bone resting thick

on the ground

ignorance flowering

while hope slips down

tina and i stripped the fence in silence

without violence

kennedia prostrata

running postman spills red fire

across the ground

shingle back lizards

slow and certain take their feast

earth offers sweetness

to those who wait

the paper purge of twenty twenty

during the first wave of covid

in twenty twenty

i thought surely this was it

surely i was going to die

my rheumatologist rang and said

stay home do not go anywhere

and i obeyed

in the barossa

we were the first region

in south australia to lock down

the news poured in from overseas

with pyres in india

army trucks in Greece

collecting the dead bodies in silence

through empty streets

the world heavy with grief

fear and silence

broken only by the calm

of nicola spurrier

explaining the restrictions

with questions and answers

and newsreaders

solemnly counting the dead

patients dying alone

families held back

by screens and distance

supermarket shelves stripped bare

toilet paper wars

the order was stay home stay away

so i turned

from the endless loop

of disaster stories

and i gathered the papers

old tax returns old bank statements

journals

written in nights of confusion

and clarity

stacked high for shredding

stacked high for release

i filled

a two hundred and forty litre bin

with the weight of my past

sent away for confidential shredding

and as the trucks collected

the fortnightly recycling

i wondered was recycling

still an essential service

would the fragments of my life

be pulped into something useful

or was it simply the ritual

of letting go

that mattered

photographs

found their way to collage

coloured scraps

became layers of new work

but journals thousands of words

pages and pages fell into that bin

burned without flame

but still burned in meaning

decluttering office heart and mind

like throwing it all into fire

symbolism of shedding skin

was there anything good in that bin

maybe   maybe not

but i will never know

and it does not matter

because i made space for breath

for life holding me

longer than i had expected

and i tell myself

i am not ready to die yet

not because of fear

but because there is still so much

to sort

eighty photograph albums to digitise

bookcases to clear

boxes of cards and letters

still whispering *not yet   not yet*

i will not go

until the work of order is done

i will not go

until the great paper purge

is complete

am I in control of that?

not entirely

we live with the illusion of control

stacking papers in boxes

shredding

what we can burn or recycle

but death does not wait

for our lists   our bins

our decluttering

still we negotiate with it

we make small bargains in silence

saying *not yet   not yet*

let me finish this one last thing

sometimes life listens

sometimes it does not

what is certain

is the tenderness of the work itself

the sorting   the letting go

the holding on

this is where our power lives

not in deciding when

but in shaping

how we live in the meantime

sophie in the kitchen

sophie at dawn fire warm on her face

bread and meat

carried the weight of grace

a hundred workers

fed from her weary hand

thirteen children growing

with the vines of the land

oscar held barrels

sophie held the flame

labour uncounted

yet the heart of their name

through rows of vines

and the smoke of day

community thrived in her quiet way

then depression fell

shadows heavy and long

two thousand palms planted

steady and strong

work for the hungry hope in the seed

seppelts sowed tomorrow

with visionary deed

© Heather Anne Gordon: 2000 April

growing older

ageing happens yet we hush it down
we whisper not me not yet not my
time the mirror is too sharp the light
too cruel our words betray the fear
we carry we say not looking our age
we say holding on to youth in a
culture that bows to the altar of
smooth skin tight faces no sag no line
no mark of living allowed

the doctors tell their story disease
decay decline bodies breaking minds
erasing the hospital is their theatre
the nursing home their stage the
script is always the same they speak
of forgetting of faltering of being less
never of being more

yet beneath these old rehearsals
another current flows women
speaking back women claiming time
as ripening not withered fruit but
fruit at its sweetest a time of travel
new skills friendships uncrowded
hours of freedom some call it release
some call it peace

but still the glare of media the glow of
screens insists that old age must be
extraordinary grandmothers riding
through cities on sleek bicycles
muscles gleaming in lycra running
marathons plunging into icy seas
silver hair polished like armour it is
another demand another weight to
carry this promise that even in ageing
we must perform

and all the while outside our windows
australia burns the air thick with
smoke our bushlands crying the
wildlife hunger the rivers running dry
the land cracking beneath the sun and
in that summer of fire women
gathered blankets tea towels buckets
of water held neighbours close when
the sky turned red and the future
looked undone

ageing through the pandemic when
the borders closed when children
could not visit nursing homes when
grandmothers waved through glass
and held phones like lifelines when
fear took root in every cough every
step in the supermarket aisles women
stitched masks and cooked meals for
others even as their own hearts grew
heavy with distance and loss

then the floods came brown waters
swallowing houses streets turning to
rivers real rivers not of metaphor but
of mud and ruin and still older women
stood in rubber boots holding shovels
feeding strangers ladling soup their
backs aching but their will unbroken

through politics shifting prime
ministers promises made and
forgotten through a referendum
where voices are asked and voices are
denied through rising costs that press
on single women retirees who count
coins at the counter who know that
glamour on social media does not pay
the rent nor warm the room in winter

still ageing is not just survival not just
loss it is also joy it is the
grandchildren's laughter across the
internet it is women gathered in halls
for craft for choir for protest it is the
story shared over cups of tea the
silence held for a friend who has gone
it is wrinkles that speak of decades it
is hands that have planted seeds it is
bodies that still reach for the ravaged
ocean even if slowly carefully step by
step

ageing is the ongoing river carrying
sorrow carrying fire smoke flood
water carrying love carrying kinship
across generations carrying gratitude
for breath for light for the simple
miracle of being alive today

mermaid wall

i was unwell bones burning with
psoriatic fire a flare that left me
crawling through weeks of near
silence yet still i dreamed mermaids
along the carport wall tile by broken
tile a rock for them to rest their
shimmering bodies

first came the blonde her mirror
turned inward eyes closed in
reflection not a siren of longing but a
quiet pulse of truth then the flame
haired sister dove deep beneath the
daikin outboard motor her scales
etched with the names of those who
carried her into being

older mermaids followed silvered and
bronzed with grey hair flowing they
laughed and spun hand in hand a
dance of age and joy and when sue
and jo arrived with food and kindness
i asked not for chores but for play
mermaid outlines traced across
newsprint their shapes a promise

and so they cut and pressed the forms
against the wall a beginning of glass
and crockery a whirlpool of mirror
water shaping life again and after my
sixtieth we gathered not for speeches
or cake but for grout our hands
pressed into the seams binding
mermaids to brick binding me back to
breath

© Heather Anne Gordon 2010 November

acacia pycnantha

golden wattle
burst of sun in winter's hand
first to greet   first to fade
carrying warmth
where frost still clings
a promise of return

© Heather Anne Gordon 2005 August

barossa bushgardens

born from absence and ache

ninety seven percent

of the land stripped bare

yet seeds once hidden

found light in open rows

the old gum four centuries strong

stood sentinel

its roots remembering

what we almost forgot

the first planting

gathered more than a hundred hearts

a paddock once empty

breathed again with promise

mulch spilled like blessings

across the wounded ground

tiny vines

reached upward to trellised light

roots whispered defiance into silence

gillian beside me

carried buckets of gum chips

even as pain

pressed heavy into my bones

every seedling mulched

was a deed of devotion

each leaf a quiet forgiveness

unfurling

our effort weaving hope into the soil

over years

the bushgardens

deepened into community

workshops blossomed

teaching ways to live gently

children learned

that caring for earth is sustainable

knowledge rooted itself

beside the seedlings

every voice

added strength

to the growing sanctuary

art found its way

into branches and blossoms

sala exhibitions

shaped by care and belonging

each piece

a witness to healing country

together

campfire

it is night time around the campfire

early nineteen eighties

i am sitting on my swag

surrounded by darkness

and the vast spiritual presence

of the land

many days exploring the country

around nipapanha

adnyamathanha guides

talking us through

the adnyamathanha stories

the creation of the landscape

the colours of the birds

one of the elders starts telling a story

about yamuti

a giant

with a pocket

to put naughty children in

is yamuti real

well   yes

scientists now know

from fossils found

in the warratyi rock shelter

that yamuti was here

more than fifty thousand years ago

adnyamathanha people know

yamuti lived

with the megafauna

here in this ancient landscape

now known as ikara-flinders ranges

and vulkathunha-gammon ranges

national park

their stories tell us so

it is here   at this meeting place

an overnight camp site

along the road from nipapanha

that i listen to the narrative

of how the world came to be

i feel the darkness wrap around me

until there is only the campfire

the gentle story telling voice

and the drift of smoke curling around

then it is time to go to sleep

to roll out my swag

to cuddle in

my back is cold

suddenly

i am frightened of the dark

something could be out there

i feel it

the yamuti story was told to us

a warning

as we sat around the campfire

and now i cannot go alone

for a toilet break

yamuti could be waiting out there

it feels unfriendly

beyond the light of the campfire

i am scared

judy   the uni lecturer

comes with me

maybe she needs the company too

the yamuti might put me in her pocket

or perhaps the yamuti will take judy

instead

mature age student that i am

i feel i ought to be braver than this

but everything

is so much older than me

i get back into my swag

i curl up

i look at the stars

i am so insignificant in this land

here is a tale about the soursob fight it
is in the front yard where the battle
ignites chooks in the back they did
their job right could i get more chooks
and fence them in but the soursobs
laughed they were ready to win the
front yard is a jungle of yellow and
green their lushness takes over and
smothers the scene tried the steamer
on a stick but it did not quite cut it so i
grabbed the gas bottle time to fire
that rocket with my flame thrower
they will soon be gone no bother i will
scorch every last one with purpose
like no other flame thrower in hand
but it is no easy feat have to bend
down low bring the fire to their feet
six hours straight melting soursobs
away only a third done but i felt okay
then i stood up arm shaky nozzle
blazing burned my wrist bad *oooh la
la* it was amazing ran cold water
cursed the pain ambo friend said *get
to the doc or you will be slain* now i
have a silver dressing and a tetanus
shot antibiotics nurse visits a whole
lot costly war but i am not deterred
scorching soursobs surely my victory
is assured so here is to the fight and
the soursobs gone in my front yard
where i stand strong natures tough
but so am i with a flame thrower and
a battle cry

figs

figs are the fattest raindrops

swollen with light

they hang like soft commas

suspended between silence and song

skin stretched tight with sweetness

ready to spill their secrets

they drop like whispers

from the branches

falling soft as breath against the earth

figs are constellations of summer

moisture stars glowing

in the dusk of the garden

they are the pulse of the soil

the rhythm of ripening

each one a tender body

belly full of sun

a hymn of abundance

a prayer answered in fruit

figs are the memory of rain

the echo of heat

the touch of the wind

as it lingers in the leaves

they are poetry

wrapped in fragile skin

they are the dance of sweetness

becoming

the promise of delight

hidden in green shadows

figs are the mysteries

the enigmas we taste

the juiciest secrets of the trees

they are the gift of the earth

offered without words

the treasure that falls quietly

into our hands

figs are the figs of our dreams

the figs of our hearts

the figs are not the figments

of our imagination

© Heather Anne Gordon: 2022 January

floating

close your eyes

feel the water rising gently

around you

it is warm at first

like a remembered embrace

then cooler   deeper

carrying you away

from the hard edges of the world

you are floating now

held

by the same current

that has cradled mermaids

for centuries

they come from everywhere

from the green north seas

and the grey atlantic

from the coral shallows

and the dark arctic ice

they have swum

in the minds of sailors

and dreamers

from the first canoe

to the steel ships of now

half woman half fish

sometimes serpent

they are the beauty

that cannot be held

the danger that cannot be ignored

listen for their voices

soft as foam sharp as a reef edge

they can soothe or they can sink

but here they choose to soothe

they have been saviour

and storm tempter and guide

and in every telling

they are transformation itself

in this land

there are brown mermaids

their scales flash like bronze

in the shadow of paperbarks

they keep the billabongs sweet

for drinking

they call the rain with their breath

they can bring blessing or flood

but to those who come with respect

they offer safe passage

through the waters of fear

see them now beside you

hair drifting like river grass

eyes calm as still pools

you breathe with them slow and deep

the air filling you

as the tide fills the bay

the hum around you

is the hum of the current

steady

ancient

without hurry

let them guide you past the threshold

into the wide quiet place beneath

where there is no dread

only the rhythm of your breath

the slow rhythm of their tails

the heartbeat of the earth and sea

you are safe here

segue

three novels waiting
notes flutter on the wall
echoes of what was paused
a segue from *desert deluge*
calling me home
the pages whisper
make us your first priority
i did not listen then
their voices too soft
but i have begun to listen again

many of the shorter verses were previously published as rage rhymes on my instagram

heather_gordon_artist_author

there are (surprisingly) some rhymes about gratitude there as well

needs vs luxuries was requested by Danette Oughton

brown mermaids was inspired by Kitty Clark (1945 – 2021)

both *andamooka* and *mermaids* were originally published in *Andamooka Anna and the Amazing Mermaids* published as an ebook by Centred in Choice in June 2024

probably rats is based on my disappointment after *possibly possums* were ruled out so when I was standing in the death aisle at Mitre10 the words *running wild in the pharmacy aisle* came to mind *Sunday* (1994) - Blossom (lyrics)

on the edge was originally published as narration for a 2023 South Australian Living Artists (SALA) online exhibition titled *Andamooka Ben and the Metal Flowers*

*driving on njadjuri and nukunu
country* was originally included in
individually crafted handmade collage
books   small gifts as apologies to
deb and barbara for my big lack of
filters

bettong came out of the research for a
series of encaustic on canvas for the
2016 South Australian Living Artists
(SALA) Festival exhibition at the
Barossa Bushgardens after reading a
Trove article "…during 1905…dealers
in Adelaide did a great trade in selling
them by the dozen at ninepence a
head for coursing on Sunday
afternoons" and "…during 1925,
Bettongia pencillata was declared
extinct in South Australia" – that's 100
years ago this year

bush turkey emerged from *Barossa
Nanna and the Twelve Turkeys*
because the twelve turkeys seemed
natural successors to *Barossa Nanna
and the Dozen Ducklings* an ebook
published by Centred in Choice in
2022

a visit to Morgan for research for
River Refuge (adult fiction) with Deb
driving and as we were approaching
the Mt Mary hotel Deb asked what I
thought about The Blue Tree Project
so I let her know and wrote a full rant
about it when I arrived home this was
the same trip that stirred the writing
for *eliza* and *lingering* and in thinking
about how the women managed in
that harsh environment my
imagination got away from me

soursobs yeah nah maybe you are
wondering how the battle continues

everyone needs to go on the
Seppeltsfield tour and learn about
sophie in the kitchen and let me know
the *basic maths* for Sophie Seppelt
giving birth 16 times between 1872 to
1891, with 13 children reaching
adulthood

yamuti was rewritten from memory
while working on a collaborative
project that included JayBee, Justine
and Auntie Judy from Nipapanha, (not
the Judy in the verse but another
auntie of JayBee and Justine) for SALA
2024 exhibited at the Burra Railway
Station

barossa bushgardens was drafted a
number of times because there have
been some highly influential people
who put a lot of effort into making it a
success, especially Chris Hall who first
invited me to participate, all the
volunteers over the years, and the
workers since that time who do an
awesome job especially Pam, Penny,
Doreen and Kim

everything else is from random
journals, although most paper
journals were sent for confidential
shredding during the great paper
purge in the first wave of covid there
were many others in folders on my
computer titled *possibly poetry* and *for
my blog when I get time* so apparently
the time might be now as I wait for
each word document to be upgraded
to the latest version